THE ADVENTURES OF
FORTUNE McCALL™

BY DERRICK FERGUSON

THE SOVEREIGN
CITY PROJECT™

PRO SE PRESS™

THE ADVENTURES OF FORTUNE McCALL
A Pro Se Press Publication

Cover Art By David L. Russell based on an illustration by Peter Cooper
Titles, Logos, Supplemental Graphics, and Book Design by Sean E. Ali

Edited by Tommy Hancock

Pro Se Productions, LLC
133 1/2 Broad Street
Batesville, AR, 72501
870-834-4022
proseproductions@earthlink.net
www.prosepulp.com

TABLE of CONTENTS

THE SOVEREIGN
CITY PROJECT™

FINDING FORTUNE

An Introduction By Tommy Hancock

Characters are interesting creatures. Part imagination, part fabrication, but largely at least a massive dose of the person who created them. To have a real believable character, I don't care if he flies and wears tights, carries a gun into the dark alleys of a shadowy city, or fights snake headed demon women on the planet Laah, the creator has to give a bit of him or herself to their creation. I mean, come on, it's been that way since the Sixth Day in the Garden.

As you delve into THE ADVENTURES OF FORTUNE MCCALL, you'll definitely see shimmers and hints of the man behind the Gambling Boat owning Adventurer. And I don't just mean that they bear a certain physical resemblance to each other. What a character looks like is a lot less important than the wind that fills his sail. And the storm of creativity that blows McCall wherever the story takes him most certainly hails from Derrick Ferguson himself.

Fortune McCall, for me anyway, has his origins tied to an event nearly fourteen years ago. Through the burgeoning wonder of the then novel internet, many writers and creators came together and started, well, writing and creating together. I met many people that I still work with today that way and many more who I've unfortunately lost touch with. One such connection I made was with a guy from Brooklyn, a guy I stumbled across by finding one his stories and turned out he tripped across who I was by doing the same. What struck me almost instantly via a chat session online no less was the voice of this man.

It would be years before I actually heard Derrick Ferguson's jovial, happy bass voice. But from the very first 'How you doin'?' in an email, I heard Derrick's voice. Strength, imagination, wild ideas, and yet a calm, an inner peace that made him different from the others in the same game around him.

I met Fortune McCall that day fourteen years ago.

What you'll find in these pages is the story of a man who knows himself. He knows his strengths, his weaknesses, his wants, his desires, his shortcomings. And he accepts every one of them with the condition that he can overcome them as he sees fit. He surrounds himself with talented people and provides a leading, yet gentle hand to those around him. He will fight for what he considers important, even if no one knows what that truly is at the time. He will stand by those closest to him and yet will tell them when they're wrong before they can convince themselves they're right. He takes in an entire situation with a glance, evaluating everything, deciding a course of action, and moving forward.

That is Fortune McCall.

That is Derrick Ferguson.

And Sovereign City? Why, that's the perfect stage for both of these men. Derrick, like the other two authors in this Project, has been able to dip his fingers all the way into the paint and splatter about till the City he needed came into view. And it's a Sovereign that ties into the fevered tales of his cohorts because Sovereign's just that kind of city. And Fortune, a man of many talents, skills, and mysteries, what better landscape for a man of his cut to walk across and leave his mark upon than one that simultaneously glistens like the future and has the tarnish of a dark past cast upon it?

What are THE ADVENTURES OF FORTUNE MCCALL? Fast Paced. Action Packed. Chock full of characters, plots, and turns that make the dead sit up and say Wow. And at the center of it all stand two men working their magic. One wears his fedora pulled rakishly down, casting a half shadow on his face, and has his hand ready to undo one of two buttons and draw his A-5 into view at the first hint of danger. The other weaves the words and sentences together that make the stories reverberate with magic. One is Derrick Ferguson. The other is Fortune McCall.

I'll leave it to you which is which.

Tommy Hancock
12/11/11

The
SCARLET
COURTESAN
of
SOVEREIGN
CITY

THE SCARLET COURTESAN OF SOVEREIGN CITY

Once Upon A Time In 1935...

Sovereign City was as good place as New York or Chicago to either hide from enemies or conduct illegal business. The entire city had been corrupt for as long as anybody who lived there could remember, ever since the still unsolved murder of old Gervaise Ravel, the last honest mayor to hold office. Not that Sovereign City was all that bad a place to live in. The schools were nothing to brag about and the rich got richer while the poor stayed poor. But then again, that was pretty much the condition all over the country. The garbage got picked up on time and the graft got paid. So all in all, it wasn't as bad as it could have been.

The collection of clip joints, bars, and warehouses along the waterfront were alight with the usual unsavory motley polyglot of rogues despite the fact that the sun had gone down not more than a short hour ago. Some of the buildings looked as if a heavy coating of grimy filth was all that held them together. The windows let in little light and considering the kinds of transactions going on inside, it was better that way.

The man sitting at a back booth of The Alabaster Flask had a stylish storm cloud grey Fortier fedora pulled low over his forehead, an ankle-length duster the exact same shade as his hat covering his black tie evening suit. He poured himself another shot of blended whisky from the bottle at his elbow and eyed the entrance warily. He plucked back the cuff of his black Italian kidskin leather glove to look at the Swiss Army Infantry watch on his left wrist. His contact was fifteen minutes late. I'll give him another five minutes and then-

The main door of the establishment swung open and conversations in the room briefly dropped to a rumbling hush as hands went to guns, no matter if they were openly holstered or hidden. The newcomer was surveyed and since he owed no one there money or hadn't produced a weapon of his own, he was not shot and he walked on to the booth in the back.

"You're late, Korbel."

Anton Korbel shrugged. "For what I have, you would have waited."

The man toyed with his shot glass. "And what exactly is it that you have?"

Korbel sat down, amusement on his swarthy face. "Ah, my friend, this is not how Anton Korbel works. You have something to show me first, do you not?"

The man held up a thick envelope. "Your money is in here. Five thousand dollars. But you don't get it until you answer a few questions."

Korbel shrugged. "Maybe I can, maybe I can't. Ask."

"There's a woman I am looking for. A woman who is very important to me. I want her back. I want to know who has her. I want you to tell me. Do so and you will have made an easy five thousand dollars."

Korbel looked impatient. "Let us be frank with each other, okay? I agreed to meet with you because I thought I could make some quick money. But the people behind your friend disappearing are too powerful for me to monkey with. You haven't been here in Sovereign that long so you don't know who you're playing with."

The man shrugged and sighed. He leaned forward. "Korbel. Listen to me carefully and closely. Because I need you to understand that I mean what I say. I'm prepared to do some seriously impolite atrocities upon your person if that will help get my friend back. I implore you not to force me to have to resort to such uncivilized behavior."

Korbel's eyes couldn't have gotten any larger. "I had heard you were a most reckless and foolish young man. Now I suppose we will have to do this the hard way." Korbel raised his voice. "Hey! HEY! Listen up, everybody!"

Conversation died as the assemblage of men and women turned to look at Korbel.

"This twit's got five thousand bucks on him. Anybody who helps me cut it out of him gets ten percent." Korbel jumped up from the table and backed away, grinning maliciously.

Men shuffled to their feet as knives and machetes, their edges glittering in the dim light, were produced. The entrance was slammed shut and secured with a thick wooden bar. Women sensuously licked their painted lips at the prospect of watching murder being done.

The man in the duster and fedora suddenly exploded into action, kicking the table over into the approaching mob. His duster only had two buttons, one at his left shoulder and the other at his left hip. The reason for that was soon obvious at it enabled him to effortlessly flip back his coat to get to the sawed off Winchester pump shotgun secreted underneath. He unsnapped it free from the leather clip on his belt. There was a leather sling attached to the walnut stock and so with a mere lithe twist of his body, the weapon slapped into his waiting hands.

He fired and blew a hole the size of a tire in the rough wooden floor. "Now, let's just everybody take it easy and we'll all go home tonight, okay?"

Somebody yelled, "You didn't tell us he was law!"

Korbel cursed loudly in French before shouting back, "He's not a cop! His name's Fortune McCall and he's nothing! Take him! He's got five thousand bucks!"

At being reminded of the money, the mob once again turned their attention back to Fortune, who was becoming increasingly aware that he was in a very difficult position. He ratcheted another shell into the barrel. "I don't want to kill anybody, but do not think I won't. My business is with Korbel."

"You can't shoot everybody in the room," a grinning Asian wielding a pair of butterfly knives offered as he advanced on Fortune.

Fortune promptly shot him right in the chest.

The body flew backwards into the mob and taking advantage of the moment of surprise and shock, Fortune dived into the crowd, striking left and right with the barrel of the shotgun, making a path right for Korbel.

The wily information broker, sensing that Fortune was a mite peeved at him, looked around for help. By this time, some members of the mob had decided to forget Fortune and take advantage to settle up old scores with enemies and soon, the bar was ringing with gunshots, screams, and curses.

Fortune ducked under a hard swung baseball bat and rammed his elbow into a stomach. He could see Korbel struggling through the crowd, heading for the men's room. No doubt he hoped to be able to scramble out a window.

The front of the bar exploded inwards as an armored black Cadillac sedan burst through the wall, scattering furniture and throwing bodies. Yowls and curses filled the air as showers of splinters buzzed through the room.

The driver's side door popped open and a diminutive black woman leaned out, the Browning automatic rifle looking ridiculously large in her tiny hands. But there was nothing ridiculous about the expert way she fired into the ceiling. She wore a leather aviator's cap and a pair of Swiss motorcycle goggles hung around her neck. "Okay, everybody just knock it off!" She yelled. "Fortune! Are you okay?"

"I'm fine, thank you for asking." Fortune dragged a struggling Korbel by his left leg. "Would you cease?" he asked Korbel mildly enough.

Korbel replied by telling Fortune exactly what he thought of Mother McCall's sexual habits with various species of canines.

McCall sighed, yanked Korbel to his feet, and cold cocked him. McCall tossed him into the Cadillac. "I hate when I let my temper get the best of me. Let's go, Tracy."

Tracy Scott climbed behind the wheel of the huge vehicle and backed out of the bar. Soon the Cadillac roared through the gloomy waterfront streets, heading for a private dock not far away. "I assume we're going back to the ship?"

"You assume correctly. Mr. Korbel has much to tell us and not a lot of time to do so."

"I told you money wouldn't work. These people are idiots. You should give him to me. I'll see that he talks."

"I'm sure you would. But how much of him would be usable after you were through? Moderation has never been one of your strong points."

The Cadillac's wheels screeched as Tracy took a corner on two wheels. McCall seemed to be privately amused at the young woman's seeming determination to crash them before they even reached their destination.

"I'll just be glad when this job is done and we can get out of this misbegotten city."

"Ah, but who says we're going to leave?"

Tracy brought the Cadillac to a bone-shuddering halt at the private dock and warehouse. McCall climbed out, hauling the unconscious Korbel out as well. As he busied himself with that chore, Tracy pressed a button on the Cadillac's dashboard. The heavy iron slab of the warehouse door rumbled open. A number of vehicles were housed there, along with a stash of weapons as well as changes of clothing and a large number of other useful items. Tracy drove the Cadillac inside and the door rumbled closed. She exited by means of a side door that she securely padlocked behind her.

Fortune tossed Korbel over his shoulder in a fireman's carry with an ease that belied his slender frame and they walked to the end of the dock. Between the two of them they bundled Korbel into a four-passenger slipper launch. There was also five eight passenger launches but those were tied up at the ship Fortune and Tracy were heading for. The ship was closed down for the night due to the current business at hand. Korbel was soon in the rear of the launch and Tracy took the wheel. Soon the launch was bouncing over the waters heading for the gambling ship The Heart of Fortune anchored precisely three and a half miles off the coast of Sovereign City.

Fortune's own heart swelled every time he looked at his pride and joy. He'd paid a little over five million dollars to have her built. It could comfortably accommodate 2,000 people, serviced by a crew of 300. The dance floor stayed busy thanks to the outstanding music of Joe 'Monarch' Redfern and his orchestra. Chefs trained in France and Italy manned the full sized kitchen, as complete as anything found in a luxury hotel. The grand casino boasted over 200 slot machines, a 200 seat bingo parlor and the patrons had further choices at games of skill: craps, roulette, blackjack, chuck-a-luck, faro and stud poker.

But not tonight. Fortune McCall had serious work to do and it could not be done when the rich and elite of Sovereign City's big rich roamed the decks of The Heart of Fortune lit up bright as New Year's Eve. No, the deeds that had to be done tonight were best done in shrouded secrecy. True, Fortune was losing a lot of revenue by closing down the ship but that was okay by him. There were definite advantages to having been born into having more money than one could spend in a lifetime

Tracy expertly brought the launch up to the ship on the starboard side. It was the work of a few minutes to get Korbel up to the deck. Most of the crew had the night off. There was only a watch on deck. A dozen hard-eyed men. They were Otwani, members of a North African tribe. Warriors hardened in both battle and in their natural land of Khusra. There was a region of that country, a brutal and harsh desert known as The Devil's Anvil. It was there that the Otwani lived and had held the land for untold generations.

Fortune and Tracy carried Korbel below decks to a secure room in the exact center of the ship, part of a series of interconnected rooms that did not appear on any official plans of the ship. There was a good reason for that. Things were kept in those rooms that would have gotten Fortune thrown into a federal jail for a long time if they were found.

Tracy lifted her nose and sniffed. The air was filled with the aromas of something truly wonderful being cooked. "Smells like Pasquale's at it again. Good. I'm starving."

"You're always starving. For someone so tiny you eat like a dockworker." Fortune lifted his voice, "Scocco! Where are you hiding?"

"I'm right here, Fortune." Ronald Scocco walked into the room, wiping his oily hands on a large red rag. Skinny as a broom handle, Ronald looked as if he wouldn't survive a hard winter in Chicago. But in his case, looks were very much deceiving. As long as Fortune had known him, Ronald had never had so much as a head cold and he had the stamina and endurance of an Arabian stallion. "I was checking over the guns, making sure they're in order."

"You checked them yesterday, didn't you?"

"I did."

"Then leave them alone. I need you for other things and I'm confident that if you say they are in order, then they are in order." Fortune cocked a thumb at Korbel. "Watch my friend over there. Soon as he comes to, you let me know. Mr. Korbel has answers I need."

From a doorway across the room, a hearty voice called, "Hey, you guys gonna spend the rest of the night jabberin' or you gonna come get some of this?"

Fortune and Tracy left Ronald with their prisoner and walked through the doorway into the armory. Pistols and machine guns of various makes were racked neatly on the walls. Boxes of ammunition and explosives were stacked with care in the corners. Four long workbenches with tools necessary for repair and maintenance of the weapons gleamed under the bright illumination. Fortune and Tracy continued through the armory into the galley.

Big, bald-headed Pasquale Zollo stood at the stove, working his culinary magic. A stained white wife beater stretched almost to bursting over his barrel chest and large gut. A .38 Smith & Wesson revolver was holstered under his left armpit. His wide face, a resume of his days as a backroom brawler, split in a grin as he said, "So how'd it go, partner?"

Fortune shrugged. "The usual. I try my best to be nice and people shoot at me."

Tracy was standing on her tiptoes over the stove, breathing in the wonderful aromas. "Oh, my goodness, Pasquale, what is all this? It smells amazing."

"Whole wheat biscuits, shrimp gumbo, green peppers stuffed with vegetables, and rice. And for dessert, lemon meringue pie."

"Where's Stephen and the men I sent with him?" Fortune asked, referring to Stephen Lapinsky, another member of his inner circle of trusted companions that referred to themselves as The Insurance Company. When they had decided on that name and why they picked it, Fortune had no idea. It was a shared joke among them that they refused to explain. He'd long ago stopped asking them why they picked that name since they burst out in laughter every time he did so and if there was anything Fortune hated, it was to be laughed at. Even by his closest friends.

"Patrolling the ship just as you ordered before you left. Making sure everything's secured and ship-shape."

"When was the last time they checked in?"

Pasquale gestured at a silver tube hooked on the wall within arm's reach. "About ten minutes ago. Said everything was fine."

Ronald's voice called from the other room, "Your guy's coming to, Fortune."

"And about time. Come along, Pasquale. Mr. Korbel might be more inclined to tell what he knows if there's an additional intimidating presence in the room."

—⋙⋘—

Stephen Lapinsky decided to take a break on the sun deck. He and the three stone faced Otwani warriors with Thompson submachine guns in their capable hands nodded as Stephen signaled to

DERRICK FERGUSON

them it was okay to smoke 'em if they had 'em.

Stephen himself fished out his pack of Morley's and shook out a cigarette. He lit it with his windproof Zippo lighter and pulled in a deep lungful of smoke while looking over the three miles of water separating the Heart of Fortune from the sparkling wonderland that was Sovereign City at night. From here it was a glittering panorama that reminded Stephen of the silent movie Metropolis which he'd seen back in '27 when it premiered in Berlin. Hard to believe that such a beautiful looking city could have the reputation for wickedness and corruption Sovereign City enjoyed. He inhaled more smoke and wondered exactly why the hell Fortune McCall had dragged him and the others halfway across the world. Not that he wouldn't walk straight into a blast furnace set on high if Fortune asked him to. That's how much he owed him. Stephen Lapinsky owed Fortune McCall much more than his life. He owed him his soul. So even though he didn't know why they were there or what for, Stephen was content to take his orders and curb his curiosity until such time when Fortune would reveal his purpose and plans.

Time to resume patrol. Stephen flicked the butt of the cigarette over the polished brass railing into the water below and turned around.

A curved silver blade pressed softly against his throat and a serious voice whispered, "Make a sound and you die."

Stephen looked over the shoulder of the man holding the blade to his Adam's apple. The three Otwani warriors were dead, lying on the sun deck in rapidly widening pools of their own blood. Whoever these guys are, they're way past being good. Lapinsky had seen what the Otwani could do and their skills were formidable. For these guys to sneak up on them and butcher them like sleeping hogs without a sound and not alert the dozen other Otwani on watch…well, that was just plain scary as all hell.

But these men…they indeed looked as if they could have sprung from some netherworld. Their tanned muscular bodies glistened from a thin sheen of water. Wildly barbaric tattoos covered their arms and legs. The man holding Stephen had additional tattoos on his cheeks which Stephen assumed denoted his leadership. He counted five of the tattooed men. Each one carried two curving scimitar like weapons that were too long to be called knives yet too short to be properly termed swords.

"We want your leader. The man McCall. You will take us to him."

"Why should I? You'll just kill me anyway. Might as well go ahead and do it now." Even as Stephen said those defiant words he cursed himself for a damned fool. The smart play would be to go ahead and do what they said, buy time, and think of a plan to either escape from them or warn Fortune and the others. But Stephen was too plain mad to care. Those men murdered were good men and deserved a better death.

"You are correct. You will die one way or another. However-"the leader's black eyes glittered with sadistic humor as he pressed the tip of his second blade uncomfortably against Stephen's genitals. "-it is up to you as to whether you die a whole man or not. Make your choice."

"Wait! Okay, you win. I'll take you to McCall."

"And be warned, my blade will not be far from your brave little soldier-" the leader pressed the tip of the sword just a little bit harder against Stephen's genitals. "-so I therefore suggest that you conduct yourself accordingly."

Stephen nodded. "There's one thing I have to do first. I'm supposed to check in every fifteen minutes. If I don't, McCall will know something's up and send somebody to look for me."

A second tattooed killer appeared as if by magic at his leader's side. "He lies!" he hissed. "He hopes to lead us into a trap!"

Stephen shrugged. "Look, I'm a dead man if I don't help you, right? So maybe if I throw in with you and help you out, maybe you just might change your mind, right?" Stephen noted the almost imperceptible glimmer in the leader's eyes as the man thought the idea over and followed it up with, "Look, I just work for McCall and he doesn't pay me enough for this. But whatever you decide, make up your mind fast. I got to get on the blower to him in another couple of minutes."

The leader was nothing if not decisive. "Very well. But say no more than you have to."

Stephen nodded and walked along the deck until reaching a door that led into one of the executive suits. Each of these rooms was equipped with a blower so that the occupants could communicate directly with the Staff Room and place orders for meals or drinks to be delivered to their suites. Stephen unhooked the tube, pulled out the cork stopper, and whistled into it.

Ten seconds later, Fortune's voice said, "Stephen?"

"Yeah, it's me, boss. Patrol's going fine. Nothing to report."

"Good. Check back in fifteen."

Stephen put the stopper back in the tube and replaced it. The leader nodded in satisfaction. "Perhaps you might come out of this alive after all. Now quickly, take us to your leader!"

—⊶⊷—

Fortune replaced the blower in its hook and turned to his companions. "Fill your hands with iron. Ronald, cut off those lights in the armory and cover me from there. Stick a rag in Korbel's mouth while you are at it. Tracy, Pasquale, hide yourselves. You know what to do."

Indeed they did. The tip off was that Stephen had spoken at all. If the patrol had been going well and there was no problem, Stephen would have simply said "Fifty-nine" which they used as their private code for 'everything is fine'. Just the fact Stephen had spoken told Fortune and the others that there was something wrong.

Fortune shucked out of his duster and suit jacket. He dropped both carelessly on a nearby table along with his fedora. His meticulously conked hair shone black as coal in the brightly harsh lighting. With his coat off the sheath on his back holding a katara was in plain sight but he didn't plan on showing it until and unless he had to. He wished he had brought along the shotgun but he'd left it in a hidden compartment in the Cadillac. His thinking was that he'd probably be going back into the city tonight and he wanted the shotgun in the car. But now it looked like the enemy was bringing the fight to him. But without his coat and hat, whoever had Stephen would see that Fortune had no visible weapons and would assume he was unarmed and had caught him unaware. Which is exactly what Fortune wanted them to think.

Fortune picked up the large wooden spoon Pasquale had been using to stir the shrimp gumbo and pretended to be totally absorbed in his task. When the tattooed men burst into the galley, he feigned being shocked and surprised, turning so that the formidable weapon sheathed on his back could not be seen by the barbaric warriors that formed a semi-circle in front of him.

Fortune looked at Stephen. "Have they harmed you, Stephen?"

"Not yet, boss. I'm hoping you'll keep it that way."

"I shall." Fortune looked at the leader. "Let him go and I'll consider doing the same for you."

"Boss...they've killed Krata and the other two!"

Fortune's dark brown eyes narrowed. "I see. That changes things. Those men were mine. Their lives were mine. It was not for anybody to take those lives except for me."

The tattooed men were plainly confused. Surely it was they who had the upper hand? They were used to their prey being fearful and pleading for their lives. But it was this lone man who acted as if he was the one preparing to deal out death.

The leader brought his blade to Stephen's throat. "Now watch another man of yours die before I take your worthless life, dog!"

Fortune said quietly, "He's yours, Tracy."

The back of the leader's head burst outwards in a spray of blood, brains, and bone as Tracy's expertly placed .45 slug entered the man's right eye and kept on going. Stephen kicked free and rolled out of the way. A split second later, Pasquale's follow-up shot doubled up the second of the tattooed warriors as it took him in the abdomen.

Fortune covered the space between him and the third of the tattooed warriors as if the metal floor was ice and he wore speed skates. The katara dagger was in his right hand and there was no emotion whatsoever on Fortune's face as he punched the broad blade right into the center of that man's chest. In one fluid motion he withdrew it and the katara dagger sliced the throat of the next tattooed warrior before the body of the man Fortune had stabbed hit the deck.

The last tattooed warrior stood dumbfounded, his blades in his hand but he was totally stunned. In as many beats of his heart, his four companions lay around him, either dead or incapacitated. There was one more gunshot, this one from Ronald that broke the warrior's right knee. He screamed in pain and rage as he went down.

"Secure this one," Fortune ordered quietly, pointing at the man Pasquale had shot. He pointed at the one with the broken knee. "I want to talk to him."

Tracy bent over the leader. "Who are these guys?"

Fortune indicated the tattoos. "If I'm not mistaken, they are members of the Ponusio tribe. They inhabit the northern mountain ranges of Greece. Very tough, very fierce fighters. Expert in stealth. If we'd given them half a chance we would probably be dead on the floor now instead of them."

"They must be part alligator as well," Stephen added. "Judging by the fact they were dripping wet when they surprised us, I'd say they swam out here."

Pasquale nodded in equal parts of grudging admiration and agreement. "Swimming three miles at night...and still able to take out three Otwani without raising the alarm…these lads were well trained."

"They had one of those blades at my throat before I knew what the hell had happened." Stephen turned to Fortune. "It's my fault they got killed. I told them to take a break. We should have finished the sweep of the ship first, made sure everything was secure-"

Fortune placed a hand on Stephen's bony shoulder, gave it a hard squeeze. "You won't make the same mistake twice."

"That doesn't bring back Krata or his fellows."

"They were warriors. They willingly and freely gave themselves over to me. By their deaths in my service, their spirits will forever sit at the feasting table of Bren. They will be buried in The Black Mountain along with their ancestors with honor and their families will be cared for all the days of their lives and want for nothing. By my blood and bones this will be done."

Pasquale hauled up the Ponusio with the broken knee and slammed him into a nearby chair. The warrior had bitten through his lower lip and blood dripped from his chin. But not a sound escaped his lips. "Time for you to talk, young man. And for your sake I hope you're a babbler. Mr. McCall likes a man who likes to talk."

Fortune nodded as he came closer. "Who sent you to kill me? Speak quickly and speak the truth. If you cooperate you have my word I'll see you are given proper medical attention and allowed to leave this ship with your life."

The Ponusio glared naked hatred at Fortune. His broken knee swollen to grotesque proportions, it must have been fiery agony. Still he did not make a sound. He let his eyes do the talking.

"Come now, fellow. I don't have all night and I still have a lot to do. I have more than a good idea of who sent you. All you need do is confirm it."

The Ponusio spat at Fortune and with a disdainful laugh sprang out of his chair with such speed it took everybody by surprise. He ran full speed into the nearest bulkhead head first.

The cracking and splintering of his neck was disgustingly loud in the galley. The meaty thump of his body hitting the deck was even louder.

It was Pasquale who broke the silence. "Now that's something you don't see everyday."

Tracy sighed. "Fortune, don't you think its past time you told us what this is all about? One minute we're anchored off Barcelona having a good time and the next thing we know you've got us steaming full speed for Sovereign City. And where's Eddie? He disappeared while we were still in Barcelona. Nobody knows where he is, if he needs help-"

"You're right, of course. It is time you knew exactly what I've gotten us into. Clean up these bodies and see to Krata and the others. I will visit with our Mr. Korbel and get whatever I can out of him. Round up Reggie and meet me in the planning room in thirty minutes."

───∞───

The grand and sprawling Mayhew estate covered well over forty acres of the Broad East section of Sovereign City. A magnificently designed estate it was, dominated by the sixty-five room mansion that had been constructed out of an exotic type of Russian marble that actually possessed luminescent properties. During the day the walls shone as if burnished with a light coating of bronze while at night the entire mansion glowed softly in the moonlight.

Gorgeously detailed marble and bronze statues decorated the carefully maintained grounds, depicting warriors with sword, spear, and shield brandished in positions of attack or defense. Although the statues looked ancient they had been carved no more than two or three years ago and artificially aged through expensive procedures.

Inside the mansion, a man addressed the two people who sat in expensive, high-backed leather chairs in a quiet library. A movie screen had been lowered from the ceiling with the touch of a button on the control panel on the massive inlaid desk. The man and the woman sitting in the chairs smoked quietly as the man shuffled through the papers he held.

Curni Asnacar moved with the calm precision of a preying mantis. His swept back silver hair and large, calm blue eyes gave him a mature, scholarly air. He always dressed in crisp blue or black suits no matter how hot or humid it got. His long, poetic face was quite handsome, if remote and cold and his long artistic fingers seemed more suited to a concert pianist or a violinist than a professional psychotic. Which is what he was.

"This is all the information I've been able to dig up on McCall and his crew." Asnacar said, motioning to the houseboy standing behind the slide projector to start showing still pictures on the movie screen.

The first picture was of a brown skinned, lean faced man with the hungry demeanor of a Doberman.

Asnacar spoke again, "You're looking at Edward Padilla. He was born in Hispaniola. Came to the United States to study law. Got his degree from Albany Law School. Supposedly he's a hell of a pilot. Well, let me amend that. All of McCall's people are supposed to be accomplished fliers. I wasn't able to find out where they were taught, though. Padilla's got a reputation for being a quick and innovative thinker. He's known in McCall's crew as being a sort of one-man rescue team when it's necessary. From what I've been reading in this file, Padilla strikes me as being more level-headed than his boss. Next picture."

This one showed a younger man, thin as a licorice whip with an engaging, devil-may-care grin.

"This boy is Ronald Scocco. Italian. A Chicago street kid abandoned by his parents, apparently. McCall appears to have unofficially adopted the boy. Says here in the report that we shouldn't underestimate him because of his appearance and age. He's hell with his hands in a fight and reads encyclopedias for fun. Next."

The next picture showed an older, bald headed man built like a pit bull with a face that testified to a hard life.

"Pasquale Zollo. Served in both the Italian and American Armed forces. Was honorably discharged from the U.S. Army with the rank of Lt. Colonel. Spent a good deal of his youth brawling in the backrooms of bars and made quite the rep for himself. He's the guy who knocked out Two Fist Twilly in a fight that went ninety rounds. McCall's got him onboard his team for his combat experience. Plus, he's supposed to be a damn good cook. He's got a wife and eight kids somewhere. I haven't been able to find out where. Be good information to know that we can use against him if we have to. Next."

The next picture was that of a man maybe fifteen years younger than Zollo with thinning brown hair, glasses, and a studious appearance.

"Dr. Stephen Lapinsky. Polish. Degrees in Medicine and Psychology. Even written a couple of books that are required reading in some universities. But don't let his egghead appearance fool you. He's just as tough as any of McCall's crew. Next."

The picture changed to show a red-haired woman with a fierce smile that was both dangerous and seductive.

"Dr. Regina Mallory. She holds degrees in physics and engineering. She's from Ireland and I suspect she might have government ties or associations with someone high up. Once my people started poking around, all information on her suddenly dried up. People stopped talking and files mysteriously disappeared. Even more than McCall and Padilla, she's the one to watch, I should think. Next."

Now the picture was of a black woman who could only be described as elfish.

"Tracy Scott. Expert in martial arts, weapons, and communications. She's more or less McCall's bodyguard. Don't let her size or her cuteness trick you into thinking she's a pushover. From what I've been able to find out about her, she's the most ruthless of the crowd and the one most likely to kill you and not lose a good night's sleep over it. Next."

The last picture was that of Fortune McCall himself.

"The man of the hour. Interesting chap, our Mr. McCall. Appeared out of nowhere five years ago with that gambling ship of his and sizable accounts in the top banks of New York, Bangkok, Barcelona, Shanghai, Paris, and Rome. The man's got money but nobody seems to know how, when, or where he acquired it. One rumor is that he's a West African warlord who went to South America and changed his face through extensive plastic surgery and is now spending the money he looted from his country. Another rumor says that he's really a New Orleans gambler who won an emerald mine in a poker game."

"I don't want to hear rumors." For the first time, one of the other people in the room spoke. It was the man. "I want to know who McCall is and why he's in Sovereign poking around in our business."

The woman sitting next to him spoke in a throaty voice, "Have drinks brought in, Curni."

"Of course." Asnacar spoke to the houseboy operating the projector "Marcus? Bring drinks immediately, please. You know what we want." The houseboy nodded and left the library quickly.

Asnacar stood back up straight, looked at the shadowed man, and continued, "I quite understand your frustration and it echoes mine. But the truth of the matter is that information on McCall is at best sketchy and at worst, contradictory. He's apparently gone through a great deal of expense and effort to keep his background murky and hidden."

The man spoke again, pointing at the picture of Fortune McCall still up on the screen. "Do you think he could be operating as an agent of the American government? That they've gotten wind of the virus I'm working on?"

"Dr. Mayhew, anything at this point is possible. But I think it more likely that your 'guest' has something to do with this."

The woman said quietly, "What has she to do with this?"

"I told you that Miss Pennington-Smythe has ties to Box 850. You didn't listen to me. Perhaps they've hired McCall to come see what has happened to her."

"Perhaps. Perhaps!" The woman's voice was brittle. "I don't want to sit here playing guessing games! I want to know what McCall is doing here in Sovereign and what he wants! My brother's virus can change the course of history and nothing must be allowed to interfere with his developing it!"

The door of the library opened quietly and Marcus walked back in, making no more sound than the cigarette smoke drifting through the air. He expertly balanced a tray of drinks and he busied himself serving the drinks, taking great care to not get into the light.

"I have an idea but you're not going to like it," Asnacar said.

"Let's hear it anyway," Dr. Mayhew insisted.

"You're having a party so why not invite McCall?"

"You're serious!"

"Deadly. Size up your enemy on your home ground. McCall would hardly be foolish enough to try anything with Sovereign City's elite in your home. This way you can get a good look at him."

"And he can get a good look at us!" Dr. Mayhew turned to the woman. "Orchid, I don't think we should entertain this idea."

"But I do think we should, Sundown. It would amuse me."

"And naturally all lesser mortals are placed on this earth solely to amuse you!"

"Watch your tone, brother dear. Don't forget who is bringing in the funds to finance your experiments. While you play in your lab all day long, Curni and I are doing the work and taking the risks. It is we who will have the say as to how to deal with this man McCall. Not you."

Dr. Mayhew sank back in his chair. He was scowly and surly but cowed.

The woman addressed Asnacar, "See to it. Have an invitation delivered by personal messenger at once. Let's indeed get a look at this Fortune McCall and see what he's about."

Having done his job, the houseboy left, closing the door firmly behind him. Once in the hallway, Eddie Padilla let out a long breath of relief. He'd been shocked as hell to see his picture as well as that of the others up on the screen when he had been summoned to operate the projector. Even though he was wearing a disguise of a wig and glasses he had painstakingly stayed out of the light so that his face could not be seen clearly by Curni Asnacar. If it had, Padilla was pretty sure he wouldn't be alive right now.

Fortune had sent Eddie on ahead days ago when Heart of Fortune was still anchored offshore of Barcelona. Fortune had charged Eddie with finding out as much as he could about the Mayhews: Dr. Sundown Mayhew and his sister Orchid. It was a stroke of luck that the Mayhews were planning a lavish birthday party for Orchid and were hiring extra help to augment their existing servant staff. Eddie had no trouble getting hired on as a waiter and as such had been able to glean a tremendous amount of information.

But now it was time to quit this masquerade and get to the ship so that he could inform Fortune. Eddie's lean face split in a smile as he thought that Orchid's invitation to Fortune would be delivered far sooner than she expected.

The planning room was a comfortable room longer than it was wide. A round table with sturdy office chairs was in the exact center of the room. A sideboard with a large pot of fresh Columbian coffee, sandwiches, and small cakes along with a generous selection of spirits occupied the far wall while a number of file cabinets stood alongside another like squat dull green sentinels.

Fortune was riffling through one of the file cabinets as his crew trooped in. Along with them was Regina Mallory, who Fortune affectionately referred to as 'Reggie'. None of the others knew exactly where Fortune and Regina had met although Tracy had it in her head that they had been lovers at one point. Regina shuffled into the room wearing a purple lounging robe with matching slippers. Fortune cocked his head at her and said in a half-amused voice, "Woke you out of your beauty sleep, did we?"

Regina went to pour herself a strong cup of coffee. "Figured somebody better grab some shuteye around here. No telling what's going to jump off tonight and since you're so damned secretive-"

"The point has already been made. Take seats, everybody." Fortune flipped 8x10 black and white photos as if they were oversized playing cards. "Pass them around while I tell you why we're here." Fortune folded his arms and said, "You all remember Tais Pennington-Smythe, I'm sure."

All of them laughed uproariously and Pasquale barked out, "Ain't not a one of us could forget Her Ladyship, that's for sure!"

"Or how she managed to leave you holding the bag in Morocco and in Athens," Regina said with a wink as she sipped her steaming hot coffee.

Fortune smiled wryly. Much as he hated to admit it, Tais Pennington-Smythe appeared to have a talent for putting one over on him. The daughter of an English lord and an Egyptian adventuress she was rich, beautiful, and cursed with a maniacal lust for danger and excitement. That lust had led her into the willing arms of Box 850 who were delighted to make use of her multiple talents in the service of Her Majesty the Queen.

"Tais is here in Sovereign City and she's in trouble. Those photos you're looking at are of The Mayhews. Dr. Sundown Mayhew and his sister Orchid."

"She's a looker," Ronald said.

"Yes, she is. She's also highly dangerous. She and her brother are both in the employ of certain highly placed German officials in this country. And considering the current leadership in power in Germany-"

"Say no more," Stephen's face was solemn. "Whatever these Mayhews are up to, if that's what Tais is working on, I want in."

Fortune's voice was equally solemn as he continued, "Dr. Mayhew is a biologist of considerable ability. For the past three years he's been working on a project known only as 'Long Noodle'. Sketchy evidence indicates that 'Long Noodle' is a virus of some sort. A deadly virus.

"Tais was sent here on behalf of her government. She befriended Orchid Mayhew and was invited to stay at their estate. But Tais suspected that the man in the third photo, Curni Asnacar, bodyguard for the Mayhews, discovered her true identity and purpose. She's been a virtual prisoner in the mansion. I'm here to get her out."

"How'd you learn she was in trouble?" Tracy asked.

"Her mother radioed me and told me what was going on. Tais couldn't contact her people for help. Part of the deal was that she takes the mission solely on her own hook. If she gets caught, they don't know her from Jean Arthur. But she told her mother about the job and told her mother that if she didn't hear from Tais by a certain date, she was to contact me."

"You're Her Ladyship's plan B, huh?"

Fortune nodded. "Looks that way. Right after I spoke to Mrs. Pennington-Smythe I pulled Eddie to the side and told him to rent a plane and fly up here to Sovereign. His assignment was to learn everything he could about the Mayhews and the city and generally be our eyes here until we arrived."

Pasquale nodded in approval. "Good deal. Eddie's had a good amount of time up here. Wouldn't surprise me in the slightest if he had already gotten her out."

"Not a chance. The Mayhews have men watching her around the clock." Eddie Padilla said from the doorway. He grinned at his friends as they got to their feet. He accepted warm hugs from Tracy and Regina, handshakes from the men.

Fortune was obviously relieved and happy to see his friend. "I was starting to get worried, Eddie."

"With good reason. It took me nearly thirty minutes to sneak out of the mansion and another hour to get off the grounds. Asnacar is positively paranoid and has men everywhere watching. Guards patrol around the clock and that's not counting this band of wild men he holds in reserve for what he calls 'special occasions'"

"Tattooed men? Wielding pairs of blades?"

Padilla's eyes glittered with interest. "How'd you know?"

"Asnacar sent five of them to kill me. They killed three Otwani before we put them down."

"Damn. I knew they were good. I didn't think they were that good." Padilla muttered. "But I don't think it was Asnacar that sent them. Probably was the brother. He thinks you should have been killed long ago."

"I thought Asnacar was in charge of such things?"

"He is but he wouldn't dare go to the bathroom unless Orchid told him he could."

"I want you to draw a complete plan of the house and grounds. The movements of the Mayhews, the patrol schedules-"

Eddie interrupted Fortune, "We don't have time for that. You're going to be getting an invitation very soon. Orchid Mayhew is having a birthday party tonight and at the last minute the suggestion was made that you be invited. Seems as if the Mayhews want to get a close-up look at the man who's been making inquires about them."

"Is that right?" Fortune grinned delightedly. "Well, perhaps the Mayhews have the right idea. Time to stop all this confounded pussyfooting around and get down to business." Fortune looked at his friends and issued sharp orders, "Scocco, get into uniform. You're going to drive. Regina, Tracy, think you can get yourself dolled up quick fast?"

Regina and Tracy exchanged mischievous grins. "I think we can clean up right smart, boss." Tracy affirmed.

"Good. Eddie, it appears you are going to have to give us the short version of that layout of the joint. It appears that we've got a party to attend."

———∞∞∞———

ortune, Regina, Tracy, and Ronald took the launch over to the private dock and Ronald went inside to get a car while Fortune and the ladies went outside. Ronald was dressed in a chauffeur's outfit. His job would be to stay with the car while Fortune and the others were inside. They would be depending on him to make sure they had a way out.

Fortune looked wonderfully handsome in his evening tuxedo but the two ladies were the ones who were really eye catching. Regina was resplendent in an original Velez Lomer black sequin evening dress. Her red hair done Veronica Lake style, with a curtain of it covering half of her face. Tracy wore a black off the shoulder jersey dress with rhinestone dangle earrings and black stiletto sandals with rhinestone anklet straps.

Fortune frowned slightly. "Where on earth did you get that dress?"

Tracy looked down at herself. The dress looked fine to her as it plainly showed that she was a highly desirable woman in a way the clothes she wore earlier hadn't. "And what's wrong with my dress? We are going to a party, are we not?"

"Why is Reggie all covered up but you're dressed like a Kansas City streetwalker?"

Tracy rolled her eyes in exasperation. "It took me an hour to get her into what she's wearing. The girl may be an engineering genius but has no fashion sense whatsoever." Tracy's head waggled back and forth without the rest of her body moving so much as a millimeter. "And as for me, I dress to please myself and what I'm wearing pleases me to no end."

"The next time I see your mother I'm going to have a lot to tell her."

"The last time I looked you were neither my father nor my husband."

"And I bless Bren for that. But I am your cousin and I promised your mother I'd make sure you stayed out of trouble."

"Ah. So that's why we're going into a mansion full of killers. You have such an odd way of keeping me out of trouble, beloved cousin."

Ronald drove their vehicle for the evening out of the warehouse. A gleaming 1930 Cord L29 town car. Elegant and dignified looking it shared one thing with the four people who climbed inside of it: The Cord was deceptive in appearance as well. From the outside one would never guess that it was a rolling fort, armored and packed with weaponry. Ronald had rebuilt the car himself and while he loathed having to sacrifice some speed there was one thing for certain: as long as they stayed inside the Cord they would stay alive.

Regina accepted Ronald's help in getting in the car, still smiling in amusement at the exchange between Fortune and Tracy. Once the car was in motion, Tracy asked, "So what's the play, boss?"

"Very simple. We find Tais. And then get her out."

"What about Mayhew and this virus?" Regina wanted to know. "Surely we can't leave it in his hands."

"We don't even know for sure if there is such a virus. Eddie said that Mayhew has a lab but he couldn't get in. Nobody except Orchid and Asnacar are allowed in." Fortune shook his head. "For tonight I'll be satisfied with just getting Tais out. Once we have her safely out of there we can make plans for a proper assault and wipe out his lab."

The disappointment on Regina's face was plain. Her scientific curiosity was in full force. But she would do as she was told. Fortune smiled at her. "How about this? When we come back for that assault I promise to let you have an hour to poke around his lab before we blow the joint to hell. I can't be fairer than that, can I?"

The three of them got to have a really good look at the nighttime Sovereign City. Ronald expertly drove the car fast enough to make good time but slowly enough that they could take in the elegant architecture of Ellington, the city's robust shipping business district. Scocco turned east on 33rd Street and was blessed with green lights most of the way toward Broad East.

Tracy was smiling. "I like this city. Reminds me of Vienna."

"I was thinking more of Prague," Regina replied. "It's kind of unusual, isn't it? An American city with such an Old World European flavor and feel?"

Fortune nodded in agreement with the both of them. "It's an interesting mixture of classicist and baroque."

"We're coming up on the Mayhew estate," Ronald called to the back. He was turning the Cord onto a wide concrete road lined on both sides by seven foot high statues of kneeling marble angels with their heads bowed and hands raised, palms turned up in a gesture of supplication.

"According to Eddie, they do like their statues," Regina chuckled. "Pretty, though."

"You think that's pretty," Ronald said. "Cast your peepers on that."

The 'that' Ronald referred to was the magnificent Mayhew mansion itself. Gigantic searchlights cast brilliant shafts of light into the star speckled night sky, sweeping back and forth. Stone cherubs balanced on wonderfully carved battlements or leaned precariously from balconies while pennants and flags snapped in the breeze.

Ronald turned into a curving lane that took them right up to the elegantly wide marble steps that led into the mansion proper. Playing his role of chauffeur to the hilt, Ronald helped Tracy and Regina out. Fortune whispered last minutes instructions into the young man's ear. Ronald touched the stingy brim of his cap in acknowledgment and climbed back behind the wheel, waving away the valet who stood nearby to park the car. There was a tent set up nearby for the chauffeurs to sit and partake of refreshments while they waited to drive their employers back home. But Ronald would drive the car himself and stay with it. He fully expected that they would be leaving a good deal faster than their arrival.

Fortune offered his arms to Tracy and Regina and the three of them climbed the stairs, noticing the number of influential, powerful people in the fields of finance, industry, entertainment, and politics who were also trooping up the stairs. Snatches of conversations filled his ears:

"...dahling, you simply must go see Victor Vail at The Croxton! The way the man plays a violin is positively arousing..."

"...heard on the radio before I came here that Machine McQueen put the kibosh on the Kiss Mahoney Gang. I know I'll sleep better at night...

"...come to think of it, what the hell is the difference between flotsam and jetsam, anyway?..."

"...you'd think that Benson would have thrown me a little something. He'd never have found those emeralds in Brazil if it hadn't been for me..."

"...I've heard that song before..."

"...just as well the Mayhews didn't invite Lazarus Gray. The man has no sense of how things are done in this town..."

"...well, sure it's entertaining but is it talent?..."

"...you really think this chap they call 'The Monster' is real?..."

Fortune nodded pleasantly at those who acknowledged his presence. There were many who did not. A significant number of who had enjoyed the hospitality of Fortune's gambling ship and had drunk champagne with him and laughed at his jokes. But here, they looked right through him as though he simply were not there. Fortune wasn't offended. Despite his wealth, his obvious culture and intelligence, he was still a Negro and therefore, even though his wealth afforded him access into company such as this, he would never be truly accepted by them. And showing up at a function such as this, even though he was invited...well, most here would treat him as a novelty and others as a bounder. And as for having a white woman on his arm...there were some here in their finery and jewels and aristocratic bearing who cheerfully would have hung Fortune from the nearest tree for such an insult to their delicate sensibilities. But the bottom line was this: he was providing them a service. An outlet to indulge themselves at night but deny in the light of day. And providing that service discreetly was armor more protective than any forged by the finest of iron workers.

Tracy gave Fortune a significant look and he knew precisely what that look meant. The kings and queens of Sovereign City were here tonight. Emperors and empresses of finance, industry, technology. She was concerned about these people maybe getting hurt or even killed if hostilities occurred. Tracy had no problem with killing. As long as the right people got killed, of course. And these weren't the right people. Fortune inclined his head slightly in acknowledgment and Tracy visibly relaxed,

Fortune, Tracy, and Regina took their places on the receiving line to be introduced to their hosts and despite Tracy's grumbling at how long the line was, it moved at a steady clip and shortly they were being formally introduced to Dr. Sundown Mayhew and his sister Orchid.

Mayhew was dressed in a tuxedo so white it was almost painful to look at him. Everything he wore was white including his white gold jewelry. The only bit of color was his slicked back jet black hair and his equally jet-black goatee, which lent his countenance a Satanic cast.

Mayhew shook Fortune's hand with exuberance. "Mr. McCall. You cannot imagine how pleased I am to have at last met the man who has caused such excitement since coming to our beloved city."

"Ah, but I suspect that whatever meager amusements I have provided are not half as entertaining as yours, my dear Doctor. If I'm not being indiscreet, what exactly is it you are a doctor of?"

"And these two lovely young ladies must be Miss Tracy Scott and Dr. Mallory." Mayhew blatantly ignored Fortune's inquiry while elegantly kissing the hands of both of them while Fortune chalked up a point for Mayhew in the plus column. Eddie had told him that Mayhew had been briefed on them all.

Fortune nodded at the man standing behind Mayhew. "And this gentleman must be Curni Asnacar. I've been looking forward to making your acquaintance, sir."

Asnacar smiled with lips thin as razor blades, his eyes never leaving McCall's as they shook hands. He didn't reply to the quip. His eyes said it all for him.

"And this is my sister, Orchid Mayhew."

Fortune had seen many beautiful women in this room but quite simply, Orchid Mayhew made them all look like twelve year old boys. A woman of Rubenesque proportions, with her Kochan stiletto heels on, she was an easy six feet tall, taller than Fortune himself and many of the men in the room and definitely taller than just about every woman there.

Her blood red evening dress sparkled slightly in the bright lights of the crystal chandeliers. Her ruby earrings, necklace, and rings were the exact shade as her hair, her lipstick, and her nails. Fortune kissed her hand gallantly. "Madame, it is most obvious to see how you acquired the appellation of 'The Scarlet Courtesan'"

Orchid Mayhew smiled knowingly. She did not take offense to the nickname and indeed, relished it. In the time she had been in Sovereign City she had distinguished herself by sleeping with the city's most powerful, influential, and wealthy men, both married and single. If there was a notable man of any distinction she hadn't slept with, it wasn't for lack of trying.

Fortune wondered if she were using some sort of exotic perfume that stimulated the male libido. He could feel a powerful sexual attraction building inside of him just standing next to Orchid Mayhew. He knew such things existed in the course of his extensive travels and had encountered women who used them. And by the way Orchid was looking at him, Fortune had the oddest feeling that she knew exactly what was going through his mind. Unlike most men, he didn't find that unnerving or disturbing at all.

Tracy gave him a nudge in the ribs. Fortune snapped out of it and said, "May I present my companions? Miss Tracy Scott and Dr. Regina Mallory."

Orchid took Fortune's arm and steered him toward the balcony, not even acknowledging the existence of the two women. "Let us take in some fresh air while we get to know each other better, shall we?"

Tracy and Regina watched them go. Tracy whispered to her friend out of the corner of her small mouth, "Would 'bitch' be too strong a word to describe her?"

"That's very odd. I felt an immediate dislike of the woman as soon as I got near her. I wonder…"

"Wonder what?"

"There's a Japanese scientist who wrote a paper a few years back speculating that some men and women give off chemical signals that we pick up by smell, affecting how we feel about them. You know how as soon as you meet somebody you either like them or dislike them? This Japanese study claimed that this chemical signal influences our endocrine balance-"

"In other words, the heifer smells good to men and lousy to women. Got it. You go keep an eye on the boss."

"What will you be doing?"

"I'm going to nose around and see if I can find that lab. Or Tais."

"Meet me right back here in fifteen. Don't get yourself killed."

∞∞∞

Fortune handed Orchid one of the two glasses of champagne he'd snagged from a waiter's tray as they bee lined to the balcony. Orchid leaned back on the balustrade, the immensity of the nighttime splendor of Sovereign City forming a breathtaking background to her beauty.

Fortune handed Orchid the champagne. "To your very good health, Orchid."

They clinked glasses. "And yours as well, Fortune. I hope we're not going to waste time impressing each other with our skill in dazzlingly witty verbal repartee."

"I suspect we would be at it most of the night if we did so. Very well. Let us 'cut to the chase' as they put it so succinctly in this country. What do you wish to know?"

"Why you are here in Sovereign City. Why you've been asking about my brother and myself. Who you're working for."

"I work for myself. And I'm here because there's a friend of mine I suspect you're holding against her will. Tais Pennington-Smythe. Produce her, let us leave in peace, and you'll never be bothered with me again."

"Now that would truly be a pity. You're such a magnetically handsome man. One full of mystery. You intrigue me."

"And on any other occasion I would indulge you to our mutual satisfaction. But Tais is a valued friend and I must put her safety and welfare above my own in this matter."

Orchid sipped more champagne. "You're working for Box 850, then."

"I have told you that I work for myself."

"You seriously can't expect me to believe that you walked in here simply to help a friend?"

Fortune sighed. "Apparently you don't have friends."

"Only my brother and Curni. Friends are an unnecessary burden. And when one has enough power, one does not require them."

"So then you don't need Miss Pennington-Smythe. As I have said, if you'll allow her to leave with me, this does not have to turn ugly."

"Hum. Apparently you intend to be boorish about the matter. Tais intrigues me. I have many games I'd like to play with her. Games I would have liked to play with you. But I think I would be better off disposing of you before you become too tiresome." Orchid fingered one of her earrings.

A rope with a noose on the end was dropped from an upper balcony around Fortune's neck and he was snatched upwards into the air.

Orchid threw her champagne glass over the balustrade and re-entered the ballroom without so much as a backwards glance.

⸻

Tais Pennington-Smythe stood near a column decorated with real climbing ivy and breathed a sigh of relief. At last she had been able to get out of sight of Curni Asnacar. But not for long. She knew it would only be a matter of minutes before Asnacar either came looking for her himself or put his men on the search. If she were going to make her move to get out of here then it had to be now.

When this job had been offered to her, she'd eagerly jumped at it. Asnacar himself was an internationally known mercenary who was wanted for crimes in at least half the countries in Europe. And Orchid Mayhew was little more than a spoiled, rich psychotic brat who indulged her unhealthy taste for blood and sadism out of nothing with more psychological complexity than plain old boredom. The real danger was her brother, Sundown Mayhew. The lethal virus he was working on was far worse than any Biblical plague and if it could do even a quarter of what she had heard Sundown brag that it could do…

"Tais?"

Tais whirled, her hands coming up in a defensive stance which she dropped immediately upon seeing it was the diminutive Tracy Scott who had found her by the simple means of circling the entire room.

"I am so glad to see you!" Tais hugged Tracy warmly. Tracy stepped back to take in the taller woman. Tais Pennington-Smythe's tan was not a result solely of lying on tropical beaches. The exotic mixtures of bloods blessed her with a natural tan that would never fade. Her bobbed platinum blonde hair was pushed back from her long, thin, aristocratic face.

"Who's here with you?"

"Ronald's outside with a fast car. Regina and Fortune are here inside with me."

Tais sighed with relief. "Then let's find them and get out of here. Now that you're here I can leave right out through the front door. Asnacar wouldn't dare make a scene with all the money and influence in this room. If I was by myself he could claim I was drunk or hopped up on dope. But with three other clear headed and plainly rational people at my side he'll have no choice but to let me go."

The two women fell into step. Thick as the crowded room was, the two women navigated through the press of bodies as if they were the only ones in the room. As they looked for Fortune, Tais explained.

"The Mayhews and Asnacar have been dropping sly little hints ever since yesterday. And I've been hearing rumors that Sundown wanted to make sure that there were 'special visitors' to pay a call to Fortune's boat."

"They did. They're dead. But why let you hear things? Why let you run around loose?"

"Because that's how crazy the Mayhews are! I don't know if they were born that way or just got progressively crazier as they got older but I've seen things inside this house that turned my stomach! Trust me on this, Tracy, we've got to get out of here and tell not only my government but yours just how dangerous Sundown and Orchid Mayhew truly are!"

Fortune was hauled up swiftly to an upper floor balcony and dragged over the railing and into Orchid's bedroom. A bedroom decorated in crimson, naturally. Several different shades of red but the effect was all the same. It was like the room entire had been dipped in blood.

Fortune's body thumped to the floor. Two Ponusio warriors stood on either side, grinning down at the apparently dead man. The third one, the one holding the rope was very pleased with himself. "Check his pockets for money and valuables. Miss Mayhew said that we could keep all we find."

The two warriors bent down greedily and that's when Fortune exploded into action, his lean body twisting sharply, one leg pistoning out and upwards to take one man in the nose while his fist delivered a stinging uppercut. Fortune's other hand reached around to yank the end of the rope out of the third warrior's hand.

In a second, Fortune was on his feet, removing the noose from around his neck. The third Ponusio gawked in open astonishment. "I've broken the necks of a dozen men with that maneuver!"

Fortune's reply was a harsh laugh of disdain. "They must indeed have been small men."

The warrior roared in anger and sprang at Fortune. Fortune nimbly sidestepped the charge, looping the noose around the warrior's right arm and pulling the noose tight.

Fortune gave the rope a mighty yank and the warrior went flying into the nearest wall with horrendous impact, accompanied by the snapping of several ribs.

Fortune let go of the rope and turned back to the two others who closed in silently for their own attack. Fortune's left arm went out and from inside the sleeve emerged a thin iron chain with a teardrop shaped weight at the end. The weight hit one warrior in his already bleeding nose, totally breaking it this time.

Fortune's other hand was also at work, removing from a padded pocket a black object the size of an egg which he flung into the eyes of the second warrior. It broke, an oily black fluid splashing over the man's eyes, nose, and mouth. Almost immediately he started yelling and wiping at the stuff. It was just enough of a distraction for Fortune to deliver a sharp, stunning right hook that spun the warrior around.

The stuff in the black egg was pure capsaicin mixed with ordinary black ink. Combined, it made for an effective defense.

Fortune yanked his chain back, whipped it out again, wrapping it around the neck of the blinded man and yanking him into his companion with the broken nose. The impact was enough to put them both out cold on the floor.

The third warrior was also out. Judging from the phlegmy rasp of his labored breathing, it sounded as if a lung had been punctured.

Fortune replaced his length of chain in the pocket of his sleeve where it stayed until needed. He checked his hair using the vanity mirror and, satisfied with his appearance, quickly and quietly left the room, considerately turning out the lights as he did so.

⸙

Regina joined Tais and Tracy as they headed for the door. "Where's Fortune?" Tracy demanded.

"I don't know! Orchid came back into the room alone. I went out on the balcony but Fortune was gone!" Regina nodded at Tracy. "Guess that puts you in charge."

Tracy nodded in acknowledgment. She was worried about her cousin but she also knew better than most that Fortune could more than take care of himself. "Tais, you stay right next to me. Regina, watch our backs."

Regina opened her clutch bag and placed her hand inside where she could get to her four barreled derringer quickly if need be. The three women continued on their way. Hurrying without hurrying, as it were. And all three women having been in combat situations before could plainly see that Curni Asnacar's men were moving into position toward them. They'd be cut off from the exit and surrounded. But still, Tracy didn't believe that they'd do anything in such a prestigious crowd.

Until Orchid Mayhew herself stepped in front of them. She was smiling and nodding at greetings from all around her. And her face was the very picture of genial hostess and her voice dripped pure honey as she said, "Unless you miserable wenches turn right around and get back to the party, things are going to turn most unpleasant."

"You can't bluff us," Tracy snarled. "Stand down before I make you lie down." The snarl was softened by a soft sneering laugh as Tracy continued. "But then again, way I hear it, lying down is something you do at the snap of a finger."

Orchid's face didn't lose its expression. An onlooker would have thought she and Tracy were sharing their favorite recipes for Dutch sherbet. "If you think I'm going to take orders from a trained monkey, you're much mistaken, my girl. I'm going to have my men drag you into the basement and give you the treatment your kind deserves. And then-"

"And then what, dear Orchid?" Fortune McCall asked as he smoothly wriggled through several of her men to stand at her side. Orchid stopped talking abruptly. She felt the prick of a dagger's tip in her side. Fortune smiled up at Orchid. The slim dagger held unseen in his hand could be thrust into her body with no effort at all as it was an excellent blade.

Curni Asnacar and Sundown Mayhew were standing behind Regina who faced them. Unseen by them, in her clutch bag, she cocked her derringer. Asnacar nodded at his men who moved in, slowly but steadily. Their eyes were coldly professional. Tais licked her lips and muttered to Tracy out of the side of her mouth, "This isn't going to end well, is it?"

Tracy muttered back, "Just run for the door when it starts."

The band suddenly burst into a brassy version of "The Lady in Red", obviously meant as a tribute to Orchid. Every eye in the room was trained on her as just about everybody in the huge ballroom turned and applauded. Everybody except for Fortune, Tracy, Regina, and Tais who took advantage of the sudden distraction to make a break for it, half-running for the exit door.

Fortune elbowed aside one of Asnacar's men while Tracy kneed the other in the groin while holding up her evening gown. The clatter of the women's heels sounded almost like gunshots as the little group ran full tilt down the stairs.

Ronald leaped into the Cord without opening the door and had the big car moving in no time at all. Fortune held open the door as the women piled in. Fortune paused just long enough to bow to Orchid

Mayhew. She stood at the top of the stairs, shouting something to her men. Fortune didn't care what she was saying as she was about to get a big surprise.

Fist sized chunks of marble were torn out of the landing and out of the wood frame of the doorway. Orchid dashed back inside, followed closely by her men who hadn't expected to be sniped at.

From their vantage points on the roofs of separate buildings a block away, Pasquale and Eddie looked through the telescopic sights of their Lee-Enfield sniper rifles with grim satisfaction as their friends drove safely away.

Three Days Later...

The Citroen Traction Avant smoothly pulled into a parking slot in front of City Hall. Ronald Scocco surveyed the street and turned to nod at Fortune McCall and Tracy Scott in the back seat. "It looks okay, but they could have a hundred cops in there waiting to arrest you, boss. You sure you want to do this?"

"And why shouldn't I, Scocco? The Mayor of Sovereign City asks for you to come by for a drink I should think it an honor."

"I still don't like it. We shoot up the Mayhew mansion and there's no fuss over it? Not even a mention on the radio or the papers?"

Fortune patted his arm. "We will be fine, Scocco. You stay with the car. If everything's okay, I will send Tracy back out. If you haven't heard from either of us in an hour, get back to the Heart of Fortune."

Fortune and Tracy got out of the car and trotted up the steps. Fortune looked dashing and elegant in his black suit with a colorful paisley vest. His black fedora was titled at precisely the right angle for him to look dashing and the highly polished black walking stick with the derby handle further added to the effect. In contrast, Tracy looked as if she were reading to jump on a horse or in an airplane at a moment's notice in her riding jodhpurs, sheepskin aviator's jacket and aviator's cap.

They were escorted right to the office of the mayor. Past hushed desk jockeys, shocked secretaries, and fuming policemen. The mayor's own personal aide, John McBurney was their escort and he seemed genuinely embarrassed by the hubbub being made.

"I assure you, Mr. McCall...Mayor Byles doesn't have a prejudiced bone in his body. This shameful display by the staff will be reported and dealt with, I assure you."

Fortune waved it away. "I expect that the staff is more used to seeing people of color enter and leave by the rear. Think no more on the matter."

Mayor Rainsford Byles had narrow gray eyes that gave nothing away as to what was going on in that keen brain behind them. He seemed extremely fit and energetic and Fortune recalled reading that Mayor Byles had been a professional polo player before going into politics.

Byles shook Fortune's hand with gusto. "Glad you could swing by to see me, Mr. McCall. Glad indeed! Please, have a seat. Your girl can wait in the other room while we talk."

Tracy said nothing, letting Fortune do all the talking and he did so. "Apologies, Mayor Byles. But Miss Scott remains with me at all times unless I say different."

"Oh. I see." But he didn't. Not really. "Then she'll partake of refreshments, then? I can have coffee and-"

"I am afraid not, sir. You see, Miss Scott's hands must not be compromised in any way."

"Oh. I see." And now he did. "Well, then, let's you and I have a good cigar and some excellent brandy and talk."

The next hour was spent in casual gentleman's talk of current events, politics, and sports. At a nod from Fortune, Tracy left to inform Ronald that everything was okay and he could relax. And that's when Mayor Byles got down to business.

"First of all, I'd like to thank you for your part in getting Miss Pennington-Smythe away from the Mayhews and putting her on a plane to Washington. She's back in Sovereign, you know."

"Really? I haven't been in touch with her since that night. I just assumed she would stay in Washington longer."

Mayor Byles blew out bluish cigar smoke. "She might have if it wasn't for the fact that the Mayhews have disappeared. When the police got around to raiding their mansion, they found the staff had been paid severance and discharged. As for the Mayhews themselves...well, they along with all their possessions as well as their man Asnacar had simply gone."

"They've left the city?"

"According to Washington, no. It would appear that the Mayhews have a serious operation going on here in Sovereign City and can't leave until it's been accomplished. Whatever it is."

"I see. So I take it that Miss Pennington-Smythe is going to try and locate them?"

"That is her assignment here, sir." Mayor Byles took a sip of his Dvin brandy and continued. "Before we continue, may I ask what your plans are? Concerning staying here in Sovereign, that is?"

"I've been enjoying a considerably good run of business since coming to your wonderful city, Mayor Byles. I see no reason to leave anytime soon."

"Then allow me to make you a proposition. I've done my homework on you and your friends, Mr. McCall. You seem to have a talent for the sort of work you indulged in at the Mayhew mansion."

Fortune causally waved a hand. "Oh, I step in from time to time to lend a hand here and there. All out of boredom, I assure you. I beg you not to associate any altruistic motives to my humble actions."

"Be that as it may. I'd consider it a personal favor if you would consent to…let's call it an informal alliance between you and this office."

Fortune helped himself to more brandy. "You intrigue me, sir. Continue."

"Sovereign City is a jewel, Mr. McCall. But a jewel that cannot shine as brightly as she should. The level of corruption in this city is astounding. For every good, honest cop walking the beat out there, I have at least three that are firmly in the pockets of the numerous crime barons who are flooding this city with vice. I've had to replace my Police Commissioner and I'm beginning to think this new one is even more crooked than the last, if such a thing is possible.

"I have no idea which politicians I can trust and which I can't. And then there are the increasing numbers of extraordinary criminals who are demonstrating scientific devices and monstrous schemes of such fiendish imagination such as would wring envy from Satan himself.

"But I've got allies. Men and women of exceptional courage and ability like you and your friends. You may have heard of some of them. Doc Daye, Lazarus Gray, Machine McQueen, 'Rocket' Mann and his Air Infantry, Aura O'Neill, The Scarf, Captain John Lawman…"

"Hardly a day goes by here in Sovereign City without hearing one or more of those names, sir. But where do I fit in?"

"This office enjoys the same sort of unofficial alliance with them that I'm offering to you. In return for certain…concessions and privileges, let's say…I would appreciate you and your friends stepping in from time to time to assist in certain matters I would not feel entirely comfortable being handled by traditional methods."

"I see. And I would be allowed to work within my own parameters?"

"I think I can trust your judgment, Mr. McCall. Do we have a deal?"

"I would have to consult my friends, of course."

"But of course. You will think about it?"

"You'll have my answer by tomorrow."

———— ∞∞∞ ————

The last few golden rays of the setting sun glittered on the inspiring sight of Sovereign City at dusk as Fortune McCall lightly walked up the steps to the Heart of Fortune's top deck to where his friends awaited.

Ronald Scocco, Pasquale Zollo, Eddie Padilla, Tracy Scott, Stephen Lapinsky and Regina Mallory were already there in their customary evening attire as they always helped their friend and employer run the gambling ship. Fortune gestured at the champagne on ice in silver buckets that rested on a nearby table. "Are we celebrating something?"

Pasquale chuckled as he reached for the first bottle. "Yeah, a life of respectability." The cork popped, arcing out and over the rail to land in the water.

"Ah, but are we meant for such a life?" Fortune said, accepting his flute of champagne from Regina. "We have become used to going wherever our whims and the waves take us. Are we ready to put down roots and become shining knights in armor defending the innocent and the downtrodden?"

"And who better than us?" Eddie replied. "We're not all that shining or all that knightly. But we know the type that the mayor was talking to you about. And we know how to deal with them."

The sounds of 'Claire De Lune' being played by Monarch Redfern and his orchestra drifted up to Fortune and his friends as they stood on the top deck, feeling the fresh evening breeze on their faces, sipping champagne and looking at Sovereign City as it slowly lit up like a city of stars.

Fortune looked at the faces of his friends as they listened to the music and looked out over the water and he knew that the same look was on his face. And he made a decision.

"Raise your glasses, friends."

"So what are we toasting to?" Tracy asked with a knowing wink.

"To us. To Sovereign City. And to the days of danger and adventure ahead."

As the music swelled and Sovereign City's lights burst into full life, seven glasses clinked together and seven laughing voices filled the night.

THE
DAY
OF THE
SILENT
DEATH

THE DAY OF THE SILENT DEATH

———— ∞ ————

Sovereign City, 1935
The First Amalgamated Savings and Trust Bank

It had been said for many years that The First Amalgamated Savings and Trust Bank was the only bank in the Unites States that one would rather dine in than do business. And that sentiment was well deserved. Tourists to Sovereign City visited the bank in record numbers as the interior reminded one more of a grand building of the Italian Renaissance rather than that of a financial institution.

On this particular morning, the bank was unusually busy, even more so for a Monday. The bank guards nodded pleasantly at familiar customers that queued up to conduct transactions or were ushered to the desks of various bank officers. There was certainly nothing different or unusual in anything any one did.

When the first body dropped to the Cosmatesque floor, two of the bank guards quickly moved in to give aid to the young woman that lay as still as if she'd been shot in the head.

"What do you think is wrong with her, Joe?" the younger bank guard asked his older co-worker.

"Dunno, Smitty. Do I look like a doc to you? I hope she's just fainted. Maybe she didn't eat breakfast. Help me get her to the break room and we'll call-"Joe Burke stopped as several more bodies dropped. Hearing meaty thuds and thumps behind him, Joe Burke turned to see even more bank customers and employees dropping to the floor as if some celestial hand had flicked their OFF switches.

"What the-"Joe Burke started to say but stopped as Smitty also fell. Joe Burke dropped to one knee, feeling for a pulse. Smitty had none. Neither did the young woman. They were dead. Just that fast.

Joe Burke stood up slowly. Dead bodies surrounded him. Dozens of them. On the floor, slumped over desks. In the space of a little over a minute, everybody in the bank was dead. Except for Joe Burke. Who now was the only living person in the building. Seemed like as good a time as any to go insane.

So that's exactly what Joe Burke did.

The Chrysler Airflow Sedan stopped at the police barricade set up a full city block away from the bank. The police were utilizing extraordinary methods of crowd control and with good reason. This was an extraordinary crime. Enough that word had spread and the mob gathered behind the barricade had grown to alarming numbers. Family members that had loved ones who worked in the bank or did business there came from all over the city to find out for themselves what was going on.

The Chrysler parked right next to a small fleet of police cars as if it belonged there. A thick necked copper bustled up to the driver's side bellowing, "Get this thing outta here! Police only parking! Your boss ain't doin' no bankin' here today!"

The driver, who looked barely old enough to drive, jerked a thumb over his shoulder at his unseen passenger. "My boss isn't here to do banking. He's been asked to help in the investigation by Mayor Byles himself. So if you'll just move that barricade-"

"I'm not movin' anythin'!" the copper shouted wrathfully. "If your boss is who I think he is then he can get out and walk to the crime scene like the rest of us!"

The driver started to say something but the cultured, resonate voice from the back said calmly, "Don't, Ronald. It is well. Tracy and I can walk. You stay with the car and we'll meet you back here when our business is done."

The rear door opened and a rapier thin man of average height climbed out. Handsome and dapper in his black business suit with colorful paisley vest, a black fedora cocked jauntily over one eye. He pointed his walking stick at the copper. "No problem against my man waiting here is there, officer?"

The policeman mumbled something inarticulate and turned away to help his fellow officers keep the rest of the crowd back as the slim man ducked under the barricade and walked toward the bank. A diminutive woman also clambered out of the car to follow him. Dressed in riding jodhpurs, sheepskin aviator's jacket and aviator's cap, she looked as if she were ready to jump in a plane and attempt to cross the Atlantic at a moment's notice. She looked equally ready to jump on the police officer. She caught up to her companion who walked as easily as if he were taking in the afternoon air along Bishop Boulevard and wasn't on his way to a horrific crime scene.

"You should get his name and report him. The Mayor's made it clear you're to be cooperated with. He sent out a special directive to all precincts stating that in explicit terms that couldn't be misunderstood. That copper-"

"-Is a human being, subject to flaws of character as are the rest of us. Did you honestly believe that a piece of paper would change the hearts and minds of men just like that?" Fortune McCall snapped his fingers. "And you're supposed to be the realist."

His cousin and bodyguard Tracy Scott snorted. "I am a realist. And what's real is that you and Mayor Byles have a deal and it's supposed to be honored!"

"Enough, Tracy. You righteous indignation is appreciated and noted."

Fortune and Tracy walked up the steps of the bank and were allowed inside. It looked like half of Sovereign City's police force had crowded into the spacious interior. They were busy at the grisly task of neatly lining up the bodies. Women on one side, men on the other. Doctors and nurses from nearby hospitals also were helping with the sorting of the bodies as well as examining them.

Chief of Police Lawrence Tate spied Fortune and strode over to him and Tracy. It wasn't easy for a man only four inches above five feet to stride but Tate did it very well. He never just walked. He strode as if he were seven feet tall. Pugnacious and sharp-witted, Tate worked his way up the ranks from rookie patrolman pounding the toughest beat in Sovereign City to Chief of Police. That might have been the reason Tate got along with Fortune and worked with him with no rancor whatsoever. Growing up in the infamous Mahoney's End slum located on Sovereign City's east side, Tate never had the time or luxury of being prejudiced.

"McCall. Miss Scott." Chief Tate shook hands with them. "The Mayor said to tell you he's going to be holding a press conference at City Hall this afternoon. He hopes we'll have something to tell him about this."

"What exactly is this, Chief?"

"About three hours ago everybody in this bank apparently just dropped dead. We've only got one survivor but he's in no condition to tell us what happened. He's been examined and the docs say that he's in a state of extreme shock. Whatever happened in this bank, whatever he saw apparently drove him right over the edge."

Tracy looked around her in horror. "Is there no clue at all as to what killed all these people?"

Chief Tate shook his head. "But we really won't know anything until we get these bodies into a morgue and the doctors can perform autopsies." Tate talked to Tracy but his eyes followed Fortune. He moved from body to body, pulling up an eyelid on this corpse, opening a mouth on that corpse and examining fingertips on yet another body.

"Mind telling me what you're doing?" Chief Tate asked.

"Just looking for signs of some exotic poison. There's only a couple of ways that this many people could have been murdered at the same time. Were any dead bodies found outside?"

"No. They were all inside."

"So whatever killed them struck them down so quickly that nobody had a chance to run outside to escape or cry for help. Given the number of people inside the bank, others had to have seen the dead fall to the floor. Their natural inclination would have been to run outside. They didn't. Which means that whatever killed all these people worked swiftly. Too swiftly for anybody to escape. You said there was only one survivor?"

"One of the bank guards. Joseph Burke. Worked here twelve years without a single incident. Good record. Got a wife and two kids. Lives over in Fort Dunham. Lives in the two-story house he was born in and moved back into after his parents died. Mortgage paid up. Has no gambling debts. Enjoys a couple of beers every night after work with his old neighborhood buddies. Bowls every Friday night with his wife, brother, sister-in-law and some friends. Never been involved with any criminal activity."

"So you're saying he's not involved in this?" Tracy asked.

"If he's not involved then why is he the only one still alive and breathing?" Chief Tate motioned for them to follow him. "Is it possible he could be faking being in shock? Faking it good enough to fool the doctors?"

"To escape answering questions, you mean?" Fortune said. "If your doctors are competent then I would say no. In any case, I will examine the man myself. I'll be able to tell if he is faking. But my guess is that he is not. Whatever killed these people...he is immune to for some reason. And it is urgent we find out what immunity he has."

"Waitamminit. You saying this is going to happen again?"

"What I am saying is that we should be ready for it to happen again. And part of that is finding out why this man Burke is not dead."

Tate had commandeered the bank manager's office as his command post. The manager certainly didn't need it any more. As Tate led Fortune and Tracy there, Fortune had another question. "How did you become aware of this situation?"

"Woman came into the bank to deposit a check. Saw all the bodies on the floor and ran out into the street as if Satan himself were trying to pinch her bottom. She ran four blocks at top speed, screaming all the way before somebody was fast enough to catch her. That's when we caught the squeal."

"So she didn't die and the first officers to respond did not die either?"

Tate shook his head in a negative. "If it was a poison gas of some kind, it had dissipated or lost it's potency by that time. Thank God for that."

"Indeed."

The bank manager's office was filled with even more police officers, captains, and lieutenants who didn't appear to be doing anything more productive than simply standing around and talking. Tate raised his voice for attention. "Hey, boys, give us the room. Take it outside. Go work for a living, willya?"

The captains and lieutenants filed out. Some with poor grace and a daring few with openly hostile looks at Fortune and Tracy. Tracy gave them hostile right back but Fortune ignored them. He took off his hat and placed it next to his cane on the huge mahogany inlaid desk. He bent over the droopy eyed man sitting in a large leather chair.

"You don't have him restrained," Fortune said.

"No need. He's docile. Just whacked right outta his gourd. I've seen hopheads with more life in their eyes than this poor boyo."

Fortune examined the man with gentle hands while Tracy watched the door and Tate watched Fortune. "Are you a doctor, McCall?"

Fortune gave Chief Tate a quick, friendly smile. "I haven't earned a medical degree, if that is what you mean. However, my father wanted my brothers and me to have as well rounded an education as possible. I know enough to know that this man isn't faking. He should be taken to a hospital and treated for acute stress reaction. With the proper care he should come out of this in a day or two. What the poor devil needs now is rest."

"I'll see he's taken to Greenfield Hospital at once. The docs have already said they want to run tests on him. He'll be under guard but I'll leave word that if you need to see him, you're to be accommodated."

"Fine. It's possible that there is some kind of immunity this man has to the poison. Whatever it is." Fortune fished out his silver Gallier hunter case pocket watch from its vest pocket and checked the time. "Is there anything more I can do here?"

"I suppose not. You know everything we do. We're going over to question Burke's wife if you'd like to come."

"I don't think so, I-" The insistent knocking at the door interrupted Fortune. The door opened and a lieutenant stuck his round face into the office.

"Got a dame out here kicking up a fuss, Chief. Says she'll only talk to you."

"For the luvva…what do you guys do when I'm not around? Get her name, take a statement and-"

"Get out of my way! I simply must speak to Chief Tate! Move, you oaf!" The slim woman that burst into the office surveyed the three with wild, coffee-colored eyes. She dressed well but looked as if she had run out of her house in a hurry.

Tracy immediately stepped between the woman and Fortune. "Hold it right there, sister. You want to tell us who you are and why you busted in here?"

"Oh, why are you all so thick-headed? I must speak to Chief Tate!"

"I'm Tate, lady. Answer Miss Scott's question. Who are you and what's your business here?"

The woman looked at Tracy and Fortune with open suspicion. Chief Tate snapped her out of it. "This is Mr. Fortune McCall and his associate, Miss Tracy Scott. They're working with the police on this. You can talk in front of them."

At the mention of his name, the woman looked directly at Fortune. "Fortune McCall! Of course! I've heard your name mentioned in Washington –"

"Lady, I'm going to have to insist you identify and explain yourself."

"I'm Doctor Christina Carver. I work at Meeker Laboratories. I've been working there for almost eight weeks now. And I think I'm responsible for those people out there being dead."

"Responsible how, Dr. Carver?"

"I'm a biologist. I worked in Washington before coming to Sovereign City. The reason I was sent down here is because for the past few years I've been working on various viral agents for possible use during wartime."

"But we're not at war with anybody," Fortune said.

"Not yet. And there are agents of foreign countries right here in America developing their own weapons. We just want to be sure that we've got a leg up."

Fortune looked a question at Tate who replied, "Meeker Laboratories has been used by the government for years now. Nobody's supposed to know about it but you try keeping a secret in this town."

Fortune nodded as Tate resumed the questioning. "So what exactly did you do and how did it kill all these people?"

"The viral agent AF29 was stolen from Meeker Laboratories sometime yesterday afternoon-"

"And you're just getting around to telling us about it now?" Tate bellowed from the depths of his barrel chest. "Lady, I'm about a horse hair shy of throwing you in the jug as accessory after the fact if you don't start singing like Caruso and tell me exactly what the hell you're playing at!"

Dr. Christina Carver sobbed in despair. "I thought I could talk to him! I thought I could get him to bring AF29 back before anybody got hurt!"

"Too late for that, Doctor," Fortune said grimly. He pointed at Joe Burke. "This man saw all those people out there die. And the shock of it has driven him right out of his mind. And he won't be the last if you do not tell us who has this AF29."

"My husband!" Christina stumbled to the nearest chair and fell, rather than sat in it. "Peter said he could sell it and get enough money to pay off his gambling debts! He owes thirty-five thousand to those gangsters! He said they would come after me if he didn't pay! So he stole AF29! But I didn't really think he'd use it and kill all these people!"

"Maybe he didn't," Fortune said. "He could have sold it yesterday or last night and whoever he sold it to tested it out on these innocent people." Fortune walked over to Christina and knelt down on one knee in front of her. "Listen to me." The quality of his voice had changed. The timbre and resonance commanded that his voice be obeyed.

The quiet authority in Fortune's voice instantly brought Christina's tear-streaked face up from the crook of her arm to look at him.

"That man over there-" Fortune pointed at Joe Burke. "For some reason he lived. If you had the proper facilities and enough time, could you find out why?"

"I-I think so…"

Fortune stood up. "Chief Tate, would you be good enough to arrange for transportation to take Dr. Carver and Mr. Burke to my private dock?"

"What the hell for?"

"I'm taking them to The Heart of Fortune, naturally."

"Now hold on, McCall…"

"Right now, Dr. Carver and Mr. Burke are the two most valuable people in the city. They need to be protected. And there's no better place to keep them safe than on my ship. It's three miles offshore which means that my men can see any attack from sea or air in enough time to mount a more than adequate defense. And I've got medical facilities on board so that Dr. Carver can run her tests." Fortune lowered his voice slightly. "And just on the off-chance that something happens to either one of them, you and your department won't be held responsible."

Chief Tate chewed on that one for about thirty seconds before answering. "Okay, they're yours. But I want two of my men to go along." Tate half turned to point at Christina. "And I want a full and complete description of your husband before you go, lady."

Christina nodded miserably.

"And what's our next move?" Tracy wanted to know.

Fortune picked up his hat and cane. "Get back to the ship and brief the others on the situation. And then turn this city inside out until we find Peter Carver and AF29. Or who he sold it to before more innocents are senselessly murdered."

⌀⌀⌀

The Heart of Fortune wasn't just home to Fortune McCall and his inner circle of trusted companions. It was also their base of operations as well as being one of the most successful gambling ships operating in that part of the world. Built to Fortune's specifications, along with assistance from Dr. Regina Mallory, a noted expert in her fields of physics and engineering, it was a floating hotel and casino. In the eight weeks since Fortune and his friends had decided to stick around, The Heart of Fortune had become a familiar sight to the citizens of Sovereign City, anchored three and a half miles out to sea.

In the center of the ship were a number of interconnected rooms that did not appear on any official plans or blueprints of the ship. There was an excellent reason for that.

One of these hidden rooms left Dr. Christina Carver slack jawed with astonishment. It was a wonderfully comprehensive laboratory. She could easily tell it had been designed to be a research lab since a physicist, a chemist, an engineer, or a biologist could have worked there with equal ease.

"Will you be able to work here, Doctor?" Fortune asked. He stepped aside as two of Tate's burliest, beefiest cops carried the unconscious Joe Burke inside the lab with a care and gentleness that belied their bulk.

"Yes…yes! This is a marvelous lab! I should have no problem." Christina looked at Fortune with caution. "Exactly who are you, Mr. McCall?"

"Exactly who you see, miss."

"I heard your name mentioned several times when I attended Diplomatic Corps functions-"

"Then I would ask you to keep whatever you heard to yourself."

Christina threw a furtive glance at the two policemen who were placing Joe Burke on a hospital gurney located on the far side of the room. She turned back to Fortune, speaking in a low, urgent voice. "I will if you promise not to hurt my husband!"

"It was never my intention to hurt him at all."

"But the police might! Or those people he owes money to! I demand that you keep him safe!" Christina gripped his arm. "Pete is a wonderful man and an excellent scientist. It's just that the gambling-"she broke off as the two police officers drew closer.

"Shall we stay here to assist, Ma'am?"

Christina looked to Fortune who answered. "Why don't you go up on the Executive Deck, officers? I will have some food and coffee sent right up to you. And perhaps a bottle of something a little stronger?" Fortune winked. "What the chief doesn't know will not hurt you, eh?"

The two officers grinned back and touched their cap brims as Fortune directed them to the Executive Deck. He then turned back to Christina. "What you're asking may not be within my power. I have no idea who your husband has been dealing with. And you should prepare yourself for the very real possibility that he could be dead even as we speak."

"I don't care! If he's dead then you have a very real problem on your hands because I want my husband brought here to your ship, alive and well! You'll see to it or I'll start talking to the press! I know enough to make them very interested and start asking questions you don't want answered!"

Fortune said nothing for a long minute. The bright lighting in the lab gave his conked hair, slicked down tightly against his skull, a metallic sheen. Then he suddenly smiled. "Of course I'll look after your husband Dr. Carver. Rest assured that I will deliver him here to you. In the meantime, you have work to do."

Christina nodded and went over to where the unconscious man lay. Fortune looked at her for about a full minute before leaving, walking through a long corridor until arriving at the Classroom. Sitting around the table were Fortune's trusted friends who not only helped him run The Heart of Fortune but also joined him in the dangerous yet heady life of dangerous adventure Fortune had chosen to live.

Along with Tracy Scott was Edward Padilla. He had come to America to study law and indeed passed the bar but that had been sometime later as he had met Fortune and his legal career had been somewhat derailed by the two of them joining the French Foreign Legion. Eddie handled most of Fortune's legal matters but these days Fortune had more use for other skills he possessed.

Ronald Scocco sat next to Eddie. Next to him on his right sat big, bullish Pasquale Zollo. The oldest and most experience of the crowd he had considerable combat experience having served in the armies of two countries. On his right sat Dr. Stephen Lapinsky, holder of degrees in medicine and psychology. Next to him sat red-haired Dr. Regina Mallory, the physicist and engineer.

"Busy morning?" Stephen asked, taking his favorite pipe, one handmade in Kenya from the inside pocket of his suit jacket.

"You have no idea." Fortune spent the next ten minutes summing up exactly what had happened at the bank and the lethalness of the missing AF29 virus.

Eddie pushed back his seat and started for the door.

"Where do you think you're going?" Fortune demanded.

"Up to the bridge to tell the captain to get us underway so we can get the hell out of here. Why? Where did you think I was going?"

"Sit back down, you. Have you forgotten so soon the deal we made with Mayor Byles?"

"Well, technically, you made that deal. And it sure as hell didn't include us getting killed by some super germ."

"Virus, Eddie," Tracy said helpfully.

"Germ, virus, what's the difference?"

"Everybody just simmer down," Fortune said, waving both hands for silence. "The mayor asked us to help and so we are. So that's that."

"What's the plan, boss?" Pasquale wanted to know.

"Dr. Carver said that her husband gambles, owed money to some people. His intention in stealing AF29 being to sell it to them to escape his debts. It could be just as simple as us finding out who he sold it to and then I will buy it from them."

"Haw," Eddie hooted. "Never happen. This town is nuts, I tell you. Chances are he sold the stuff to a real loony. Why else would they kill all those people? They wanted to make sure it did what Carver claimed it could do. That means whoever has it doesn't give a poobah's pizzle who he kills or how many."

"We still have to try, right, Fortune?" Regina said.

"Right. So here's what we are going to do: Tracy and Scocco, you'll come with me. Reggie and Eddie, you will work together. We're going to comb all the gambling spots, spread some paper, ask some questions. Find out who Carver owed. Once we find them, we will link up togcthcr and approach them. Could be we'll have to take it by force. But take it we shall." Fortune pointed at Stephen. "You are a medical man, Stephen. You'll stay to assist Dr. Carver should she need assistance."

"Just as you say, Fortune."

"Pasquale, you're in charge while we are ashore. Once we leave the ship I want you to have lookouts with strong binoculars fore, aft. Rotate the lookout every three hours. Regular patrols until I get back on board."

"What are they looking for?"

"I'm going to take along a flare gun. If they report seeing a red flare, you bring along a dozen well armed Otwani and report to Chief Tate. By then, I will have gotten word to Tate where I want you."

Pasquale saluted in response. Fortune gestured at Tracy, Ronald, Regina, and Eddie. "Get weapons and whatever else you need. Meet me at the launch in ten minutes. Oh…and Stephen, may I have a word with you? There's a certain issue regarding our Dr. Carver I may need you to address…"

⎯ ☙⊗❧ ⎯

Mozelle Miezekowski certainly didn't look anything like what a crime lord (or in her case, crime lady) was supposed to look like. Short, generously rounded with very pale skin, heavenly gray eyes

THE DAY OF THE SILENT DEATH

and luxurious sand colored hair she looked more like a movie star. On looks alone she could easily have given Davis or Harlow a run for their money. Nonetheless, she was the undisputed boss of anything criminal that took place in Sovereign City's east side from East 44th Street all the way up to Damaris Square in the Hillside section.

How she maintained her power wasn't a secret. In fact, Mozelle quite liked it that everybody in Sovereign City knew The Overstreet Association backed her. And the story of how she got them to back her was one she had never seen fit to share with any one. Rumor had it she was the wife, sister, or daughter of an Association member. If so, she wasn't telling and ever since Louis DeRosa had been hauled out of the river eight years ago missing his tongue and ears after he had been so ungentlemanly to ask, nobody dared to inquire a second time.

The respectful knock on her office door made her look up from her bookkeeping in annoyance. Her people knew she set aside a certain time every day for this and she shouldn't be disturbed. "Come in!"

Her second-in-command, Sammy September opened the door and stuck his towhead in. "You're not gonna believe who's here. That fancy darkie what runs the gambling ship."

"You must be joking. McCall? Here? What does he want?"

September shrugged his shoulders. "Wouldn't tell me. Just said it could be financially beneficial to you. I told him to take it on the dangle. Then he said he'd pay five hundred bucks for fifteen minutes of your time."

"What?"

"No joke. Reached inside a pocket and pulled it out like he does it everyday. I told him to wait. What do you want to do?"

"Is he alone?"

"Nah. Got a doll with him. Dunno what she is to him but she's a cute trick for a darkie. So what do you want to-hey!"

September stumbled inside the room, propelled by a firm shove from Fortune who stepped into the room along with Tracy. She closed the door and put her back to it, the pair of .45 automatics gleaming in her small hands as she pointed them at the furious September. "Just take a seat, big boy. We won't be here long so there's no reason this has to turn bloody."

Mozelle sized up Fortune who had garbed himself in his stylish

Fortier fedora, calf length duster and gloves, all the exact shade of storm cloud gray. His trench coat only had two buttons, one at his left shoulder and the other at his left hip. The reason for that is that it enabled him if necessary to effortlessly flip back his coat to get to the sawed off Browning A-5 pump shotgun secreted underneath. A custom made leather harness fitted over his shoulders under the coat to support the fearsome weapon and a lanyard attached to the walnut stock. The rest of the weapon clipped to Fortune's belt. Fortune had spent many hours practicing with the thing and had gotten so proficient that with a mere lithe twist of his body the weapon snapped free of the clip and could be slung right into his waiting hands.

"Miss Miezekowski." Fortune removed his fedora elegantly and bowed with a flourish. "Forgive this intrusion. I personally detest being rude but the urgency of the situation I currently find myself in forces me to sacrifice the courtesies I would normally observe. Especially with a woman of your reputation."

Mozelle sat back in her chair, reaching for a French made cigarette she placed in an amber cigarette holder. Her gray eyes were plainly intrigued. "Sit down, Mr. McCall."

"Please, call me Fortune." He stepped forward to light her cigarette with a solid gold Fernlund lighter he seemingly produced from thin air.

Mozelle took in a deep lungful of smoke. Let it dribble out through her full lips and inhaling it back in through her nose. "I think I like you, Fortune. You have manners. Manners are so rare to find in this business of mine."

Behind Fortune, unseen by Mozelle, Tracy rolled her eyes in exaggerated disgust.

"How did you get past Sammy's men?" Mozelle wanted to know.

"I regret to inform you that several of them will not be able to finish out their work day. I assure you none of them are permanently damaged. But first things first." Fortune reached into a pocket of his coat and took out a roll of bills secured with a rubber band. He placed it on Mozelle's desk. "Five hundred dollars for fifteen minutes."

"You've bought your time."

"You heard what happened at the First Amalgamated Bank this morning?"

"Who hasn't? That's all that's been on the radio."

"I'm looking for a man named Peter Carver. He is involved and he may cause it to happen again."

Mozelle was even more intrigued now. "How?"

"A lethal virus. Deadly in the extreme. Carver's wife told me that Peter has a very bad gambling habit and owes thirty-five thousand. I was hoping you could tell me who holds his marker and where I can find them."

Mozelle asked slyly, "What makes you think I don't?"

"Do you?"

Mozelle said to September, "Sammy, do we know this Carver?"

"We used to. I stopped him from coming in here about three weeks ago. I heard about that scratch he owes. I didn't want his business here and told him so."

"Word about Carver travels fast, eh?"

"Hey, owing Sonny Terwilliger thirty-five thousand is a big deal in this town, buddy."

Fortune looked from September to Mozelle. "I've heard of this Terwilliger."

Mozelle smiled as she blew out cigarette smoke. "He's certainly heard of you. He's got a standing offer to pay twenty-five thousand dollars to anybody who blows up your pretty shiny ship."

"Sounds like Mr. Terwilliger is just the man I should be seeing then. I'll trouble you no more, Miss Miezekowski." Fortune replaced his hat upon his head and turned sharply, his coat billowing slightly. "Tracy, say goodbye to Mr. September."

"Goodbye, Mr. September." Tracy slipped one automatic into a shoulder holster and opened the door for Fortune, keeping the other one trained firmly on the seething Sammy September.

"Fortune!" Mozelle called. Fortune stopped and half turned back.

"Drop back by for a drink when you've completed your business. Leave your little friend at home."

Fortune smiled. Touched the brim of his hat in salute. Turned to go. Tracy was right behind him, closing the door firmly. They walked through Mozelle's gambling den, stepping over the still unconscious bodies of the men who had tried to stop them.

"You wanna flirt on your own time? We're busy people, y'know." Tracy grumbled.

"Isn't it so much easier to get information by simply talking to people in a civilized manner?"

Tracy suddenly whirled around, her .45's coming out of their holsters with frightening speed. The boom of the two guns filled the air as she fired at the door jamb of Mozelle's office, driving Sammy September back inside, dropping his revolver in shock. The door slammed shut but Tracy continued to pound slugs into the door, knocking fist sized holes in it.

Tracy stowed her guns back into their holsters. "Depends on the people you're talking to, cousin."

⸺∞⸺

Regina Mallory sat in a twin to the Chrysler Airflow Sedan Fortune Tracy and Ronald were using. And like that one, this car was armored. Complete with bullet proof glass and puncture resistant tires. An alarming number of weapons reposed in hidden compartments. And they could stay in contact with the other car or call The Heart of Fortune by means of the shortwave radio built into the dashboard.

Regina casually smoked a cigarette as she read the latest issue of Mechanical Engineering Monthly. Eddie was off asking questions about their quarry. Both of them had agreed it would probably be better for Regina to stay in the car.

Sovereign City, like most cities of the world was made up of neighborhoods. And most of those neighborhoods tended to be inhabited and populated along cultural and racial lines. This was why it was Eddie who had suggested he alone make the inquiries in Little Madrid, the barrio containing most of Sovereign City's Latino citizens. Many of the people living here worked as domestics, janitors, porters, and cleaners for the wealthy and powerful. And they heard much and saw more as they went about their work. It was a resource Eddie Padilla had been quick to make use of in the time they'd been here in Sovereign City.

Regina turned the page, looked up and around to give the street the once over as she sat there. Washing hung out to dry on fire escapes and on clotheslines strung between the buildings. Men and women sat or stood on their stoops, chatting and passing the time of day. Hard to realize that just a few short hours ago mass murder had been committed and might happen again.

Regina looked at the imposing Daye Tower that could be seen from just about anywhere in Sovereign City. As an engineer, Regina could appreciate the work that had gone into the design and architecture of the magnificent spire. As a woman she delighted in not only the form and design of the building but its sheer beauty.

Eddie opened the driver's side door and slid into the seat. "Thanks for waiting, Regina. Hope you're not too offended."

"I'm not offended at all, Eddie. Don't be silly." And she wasn't. Regina knew full well that in neighborhoods like this, a strange white face, male or female was oftentimes cause for alarm, suspicion, fear and even anger. If she had gone with Eddie, nobody would have talked to him. On his own he could operate much better. "So what did you get?"

"I talked to a couple of guys who said that a white guy put out the word he had something big to sell. Something that would make whoever owned it king of Sovereign City. He was asking a hundred large for whatever it was. But after that initial offer, nothing. Nobody knows what happened to him."

"You think somebody bought the AF29 from him?"

Eddie shrugged as he started up the car. "Either that or they killed him for it. You ask me, this is a fool's mission. We ought to all stay on the ship and wait for this situation to play itself out."

"You know that's not going to happen," Regina laughed as Eddie merged smoothly into traffic. "So where do we go to now?"

"I say we head on over to the east side. Fortune's working the west. Let's see what we can pick up there. You checked in with Fortune?"

"About ten minutes ago. He said the police have torn Carver's place to splinters and found nothing. He got a name, however: Terwilliger. He's going to check it out and said he'd call if he needed us."

The radio crackled for attention. Regina picked up the microphone, thumbed the button on the side to talk. "Regina here. Go ahead."

"It's Pasquale, Regina. Guy just called up the ship by radiophone. Wouldn't give a name. Said he heard that Fortune is looking for Carver. Guy claims he knows where Carver is."

"You told Fortune?"

"Sure. He said he's following up a lead and to throw it to you and Eddie. So I'm throwin'."

"In that case, we're catching. Got an address?"

"11 East 49th Street between Spring and Maccaro. Apartment #5."

Regina said, "Got it. We'll let you know if it pans out." She replaced the microphone and said to Eddie, "Hit it."

Thanks to the supercharged, finely tuned engine and Eddie's expert driving they were soon at their destination. The street was located within walking distance of the busy Tilly Plaza and so was a mixture of residential and business. 11 East 49th itself turned out to be an eleven story apartment building. Not affluent enough for a doorman but it did have an intercom system. Regina thumbed #5. Nothing. No response. She thumbed again. Still nothing.

"Lay off that, willya?" Eddie insisted. "C'mon." He pushed open the door and held it for Regina as she walked in, her heels clicking on the decorative tile floor.

"Did you just pick that lock?"

"Sure I did. Did you think I was going to wait all day for you to finish fooling around with that buzzer?" Eddie took her elbow, steered her toward the elevators.

"Eddie, we're expected."

"Just because we're expected doesn't mean we're welcome," Eddie insisted as the elevator doors opened. He consulted an apartment directory and pressed the appropriate floor.

"Your problem is you think like a criminal."

"Your problem is you don't. Why do you think Fortune keeps me around?"

"He told me once it's because you make him laugh. You remind him to keep a sense of humor."

"And here I thought I was just another pretty face."

The elevator doors opened and they stepped into the long hallway. Eddie looked at the numbers on the nearest apartment doors. He pointed. "Gotta be down that way."

As they walked in that direction, an apartment door opened and a bespectacled man came out of apartment #5, holding a large leather satchel.

"Excuse me!" Regina called. "I think you're-"the rest of her greeting was cut off by Eddie shoving her to one side of the corridor even as he threw himself to the other side. Mainly because the bespectacled man whipped out a large revolver and began enthusiastically pegging shots their way.

Regina's small hand dived in her purse and came out with her four barreled derringer. She fired twice but hit nothing but air as the man sprang back into the apartment, slamming the door shut.

Eddie had scrambled to his feet, helping Regina up. "He's gonna go for the fire escape! You keep him busy while I get downstairs!" Eddie charged for the staircase while Regina ran to the apartment door. It opened easily when she pushed it. She ran inside, derringer at the ready. She heard the clattering of feet on the metal fire escape and ran to the bedroom.

She looked out the open window. The spectacled man was already three floors down. Regina fired two shots but at that distance her derringer was useless. She pulled her head back in as the bespectacled man fired two shots of his own up at her with his weapon which most certainly had more power and range. She popped her head out long enough to yell, "He's on his way down to you, Eddie!" then ducked back in as another bullet zinged upwards.

She turned around and headed out back through the bedroom into the living room. Eddie could take care of himself and even now she heard gunshots being exchanged. The best thing to do now would be to search the apartment and see what she could come up with.

It didn't take her long. In the living room, behind a couch where it had been rolled out of sight was a body. After turning it over and checking his pulse Regina verified it was a dead body. Of a man. Maybe in his late forties and from the expression on his face, very much surprised to be dead. "Damn." She checked his pockets and found his wallet.

Eddie came into the apartment. Alone.

"Where's the guy?" Regina wanted to know.

"Got away. Whoever he is, he can run. He made it to the corner and by the time I got there, he was gone. And I do mean gone. Maybe he ducked in a building or down an alley."

"So why didn't you go after him?"

"Didn't want to leave you alone in case he had a buddy hanging back. Who's this? Carver?"

Regina shook her head. "Doesn't fit the description Fortune gave us. His driver's license says he's Abel Hardy. This is his apartment. I wish you hadn't let that guy get away, Eddie. He might have been carrying AF29 in that satchel."

"In that case, I'm glad he got away. What makes you think I want to catch a guy toting around a bag full of killer germs?"

Regina flashed him a smile of amusement. "You're really scared of germs, aren't you?"

"I've never had so much as a cold in my life and I don't intend to get taken out by a hopped-up flu virus. Let's get back to the car and report to Fortune."

"Shouldn't we call the police?"

"After we report to Fortune and we're in the car six blocks away. You want to spend the rest of the day answering dumb questions and miss out on the action?"

Sonny Terwilliger occupied the penthouse suite of the Remick Hotel, one of the most expensive and swankiest hotels in Sovereign City. One had to make a reservation up a year to get a room in the Remick. Any room. What would have been a luxury room in any other hotel were the basic accommodations in The Remick.

Fortune and Tracy entered the cavernous lobby of the Remick Hotel. So high up was the ceiling Tracy could have sworn clouds were forming up there. The immense marble columns were as thick around as sequoia trees. A desk clerk smiled helpfully at Fortune. "Good afternoon, Mr. McCall. How may I help you?"

The always suspicious Tracy had a question of her own first. "How do you know who he is?"

The desk clerk's smile increased. "The staff of the Remick Hotel makes it our business to know all of Sovereign City's famous and influential citizens, Miss Scott. And in the short time Mr. McCall and his associates have been here you most certainly have become citizens worth extra notice."

If the situation hadn't been so serious, Fortune would have enjoyed seeing Tracy flabbergasted. It wasn't often that she was caught flat-footed with nothing to say. "I'm here to see Mr. Terwilliger if he is in."

"Let me check, sir. Mr. Terwilliger has his own private elevator to the garage and so does not have to come through the lobby to enter and leave the hotel. Excuse me." The desk clerk turned away and walked toward the switchboard room.

Fortune gestured at Tracy, who followed him without a word. She knew what he was up to. It didn't take them long to find the penthouse's private elevator. Fortune reached into a pocket of his coat and withdrew a small leather case which held lock picks. It was the work of less than a minute to get the doors open. They stepped inside the elevator and Fortune took hold of the controller, sending the elevator speeding upwards.

It took maybe two minutes for the elevator to arrive at its destination. The doors slid open. Fortune and Tracy stepped out and stood still as they took in the scene.

The beauty of the penthouse apartment went unnoticed by the pair due to the number of dead bodies lying around. Several of them sitting in chairs and on the couches, the smashed glasses and puddles of liquid on the polished floor indicating that they had died while holding drinks in their hands.

Tracy let out a small yelp, covered her mouth and nose with her hand, and jumped back into the elevator. "Fortune! Let's get out of here!"

Fortune seized her by the shoulder. "We're okay. That infernal virus is so lethal that if it were still potent we would have dropped dead the very instant we stepped out of that elevator."

Tracy stepped back into the penthouse apartment. Gingerly. Lowered her hand very slowly. When she didn't drop dead she let out the breath she'd been holding. "From now on, we go nowhere without gas masks. And we put them on before entering a room or a building we don't know is safe."

"Agreed." Fortune moved among the male and female bodies. "There has to be at least a dozen dead here. Which one is Terwilliger, I wonder?"

"This is him." Tracy stood behind the bar and waved for Fortune to come on over. A man of average height lay there, dressed like the other men in a business suit so new he might have bought it that morning.

"How do you know?" Fortune asked.

Tracy indicated the scars at the corners of his mouth. They were old scars but still very noticeable. "They call that a Glasgow smile. Terwilliger spent some time in England when he was younger running with the London mobs. That's where he picked that up."

Fortune and Tracy looked up upon hearing the sounds of another elevator. The two of them followed the sound to the spacious kitchen. It had its own service elevator used by the hotel staff to bring meals up directly from the hotel kitchen. Also, when the penthouse resident had parties, the staff could use the elevator to quickly and quietly ferry whatever was needed back and forth.

Tracy reached for her guns but Fortune shook his head in a negative. "You won't be needing that. Unless I'm very wrong, that would be Chief Tate and a small army of police officers on their way up."

"How can you be sure?"

"Once we disappeared so suspiciously, I'm sure that the desk clerk called the house detective who called the police. Once my name was mentioned, that information was relayed to Chief Tate who made it his business to get here as quickly as he could to see for himself what we've learned."

Indeed, Fortune was correct. The service elevator doors split apart and Chief Tate bustled out at the head of a small army of grim faced officers with their guns drawn. "Fortune! What the blazes is going on up here! I got a call from the hotel dick who said you'd broken into a private elevator! They thought you were coming up here to blast Sonny Terwilliger!"

"Now why would I want to do that, Chief?"

"Gimme a break! Everybody knows that Terwilliger wanted your ship blown up. Now what are you doing here?"

Fortune motioned for Tate to follow him back into the penthouse proper. Tate's eyes opened as wide as they could upon seeing the grotesque scene before him. "Holy Jumpin' Hanna! We're gonna have to build a whole new morgue if this keeps up! The same stuff got them, eh?"

Fortune removed his fedora, held it in his gloved hands as he nodded. "No other signs of violence. Undoubtedly AF29."

"So let me get this straight: Carver comes up here, doses Terwilliger with the stuff?"

"Be the most expedient way of eliminating his debt, don't you think?"

"So we've still got Carver running around with the stuff. And according to his wife he took a dozen vials. So assuming he used one at the bank and another here, he's still got ten left. More than enough to kill a whole lot of folks unless we stop him."

"You have accurately summed up our dire situation most succulently, Chief." Fortune replaced his fedora on his head. "Come, Tracy."

"Hey! Where are you going now?"

Fortune half turned. "As you said, Peter Carver still has ten vials of death in his possession. I'm going back out there on the street and try to find him before he either leaves the city or leaves more dead bodies for us to clean up."

———

Peter Carver could no longer feel his arms or legs and his bladder had long ago given up the fight. His arms and legs were completely numb and the urine soaking his pants had turned cold. It didn't help that he was locked inside a damp, chilly basement. The chair his captor had tied him to was too wide for him to tip over. He had tried. But nothing he did budged either the chair or the ropes in the slightest.

He had no idea how long he'd been here. A day at least. His captor had taken great care to cover the basement windows with oilcloth to keep out the sunlight. But judging from the way his stomach was rumbling, Carver estimated it had been a day since he'd last eaten. And his mouth was so horribly dry.

The basement door opened swiftly and closed in the same manner. A minute passed as Carver's captor made his way to a table and the kerosene lamp resting on it which he lit, illuminating the basement. It baffled Carver how the man could walk so unerringly from the door to the table in absolute darkness and not bump into it.

His captor set a large leather satchel on the table. He wore glasses that he did not need to see but they were useful as a disguise. People tended to focus on the glasses and not on the face behind them.

"Water!" Carver croaked. "Please."

"But of course," his captor said most reasonably. He walked out of Carver's line of sight and Carver heard the sound of water running and splashing in a sink. Shortly, the man returned with a glass of water which he put to Carver's lips. Carver drank greedily. Never had water tasted as good or as sweet. It took three more glasses before his thirst was quenched.

His captor sat down at the table, removed his glasses and crossed his legs. "Well, you'll be happy to know at AF29 works exactly as you said it would, old fruit. I'm jolly well pleased. You'll be less happy to know that Sovereign City's entire police department is turning the town upside down looking for you."

"Me? Why?"

"You've been a busy boy. You've killed almost a hundred people today between the bank and Sonny Terwilliger's penthouse. The police have orders to shoot you on sight."

"You did it!"

"Well, of course I did. I had to be sure that AF29 worked, didn't I? The only way to do that was to test it out in the field. You should be proud. But it needs another name. AF29 is so cold, so clinical. It's got no verve, no va-voom! Know what I mean, old fruit?" The man grinned amiably at Carver as if they were talking baseball and not mass murder. "I'm thinking of renaming it The Silent Death. What do you think? Too cliché?"

"You're insane!"

"Guilty. But I knew that when I killed my parents on my eighteenth birthday. Best present I could have given myself as then I was of legal age to take control of the fortune my father had built up thanks to his copper mine."

"Who are you?"

"I suppose it does no harm to properly introduce myself. Lamido Sanusi, at your service."

"What do you want from me?"

"I already have it, old fruit." Sanusi reached out a hand to pat the leather satchel as if it were an old and faithful hound. "Thanks to your loose lips I have the means to kill hundreds, if not thousands."

"But...but why? For what possible reason could you have for wanting to kill people who never did you any harm?"

Sanusi threw back his head and a well-modulated laugh erupted from his throat. It was all very theatrically done, as if he were laughing because it was expected that he laugh at this point, rather than him truly feeling amusement at what had been said.

"Well, it's like this…there's this…well, it's a sort of group, actually. The requirements for membership are extremely stringent and somewhat rigid, if you ask me. But then again, what's the point of joining an organization that will just let anybody join? You must understand, old fruit."

"Stop calling me that! And you're willing to murder hundreds just to join this…this club?"

"You have to trust me on this. The Assembly of Masks is not just a club. And to join them you have to be much, much more than your everyday, run of the mill murderer…"

———⚬⚬⚬———

Eddie and Regina pulled their car up next to Fortune's. He stood next to the vehicle along with Tracy and Ronald, both of who were munching on sandwiches and cold fried chicken thoughtfully provided by Pasquale. Quart jars of sparkling iced tea rested on the roof of the car.

Fortune waved a hand. "Help yourselves," he said absently. He stood staring off into the skyline of Sovereign City.

They were parked on a hill located inside of Osbourne Park. Fortune had used his car's radio to contact Eddie and Regina so they could all meet up, exchange notes, and figure out what to do next.

Around a mouthful of chicken leg, Eddie said, "Aren't you going to eat, Fortune?"

Tracy caught Eddie's eyes and shook her head. "I tried. You know how he gets when he's on the hunt. He doesn't eat, doesn't sleep…"

"A condition you obviously don't suffer from," Regina said to Ronald Scocco who was on his fourth turkey sandwich.

"I'm a growing boy," Ronald replied with such a deadpan expression Regina couldn't tell if he was pulling her leg or not.

"Fortune? What's our next move?"

"We go back and question the wife. She has to know more than she's telling us. If necessary we will use chemical coercion to make her tell us. The stakes are too high here for us to fail."

"You're forgetting that you've got a ship," Eddie said. "You can just get on and sail away. Leave this mess behind."

"Edward, we are not leaving and I'm weary of continually hearing that suggestion from you. Either offer constructive ideas to solve the current problem or return to the ship and stay there."

Just the fact that Fortune had called him by his full name and not the usual 'Eddie' said to Eddie that maybe he was pushing it a bit much. He fell silent and ate his food while Fortune resumed talking, gloved hands clasped behind his back, the freshening mid-afternoon air flapping at his coat.

"We are operating on the premise that the bespectacled man who shot at you has the AF29, correct?"

"Correct."

"Who was the man he killed?"

"Abel Hardy." Regina passed over the dead man's wallet. "Eddie says he's heard of him."

"Guy was an information broker. Traded, bought, and sold information both legal and illegal. Made a pretty good living from it. I've never used him since we've been here in Sovereign City but his name was mentioned to me several times and I filed his name away as a possible source should we ever need it."

"Could it be that Abel was acting as the go between for Carver and the bespectacled man? Perhaps for a sale?"

"And the guy with the glasses decided to cut out the middle man and avoid paying the hundred large." Eddie nodded. "I like it."

"How do we find out who that guy with the glasses is?" Ronald wanted to know.

"That is the question. If his wife can't point us in the right direction-"

"What about the people who worked with them in the lab? We haven't talked to them yet." Tracy said.

"I believe the police rounded them all up and spoke to them but it wouldn't hurt for us to talk to them. Tracy, call Tate and get names and addresses. Finish up eating and let's get moving."

Stephen Lapinsky re-entered the laboratory aboard the Heart of Fortune. Christina Carver had spent most of the day running tests on blood taken from the unconscious Joe Burke. With his help she isolated what she was positive was the active agent in his metabolism that kept him alive during that morning's horrific attack.

She smiled at Stephen as he came closer. Stephen bore a covered silver tray. He placed it on a nearby workbench and lifted off the cover. "Steak and potatoes, doctor. Not the finest of cuisines you'll find here on board the Heart of Fortune but right now I'm guessing you don't want anything fancy. Just filling."

"You're so very right, Mr. Lapinsky. Thank you." Christina pulled up a stool and dug into her food with the vigor of a dockworker. "First real meal I've had all day long."

"I've just heard from Fortune. He radioed me from the city."

Christina looked up, a forkful of steak halfway to her mouth. "Has he found Peter? Is he all right? Is McCall bringing him here?"

"No, he hasn't found him. Not yet. He's still looking but he wants to know if you know anywhere he would have gone…any one who would give him a place to stay, lend him money."

"I didn't socialize with those people. Those were Peter's friends. I told him to stay away from them but he wouldn't listen! That's how he ended up in this mess! Those people probably cheated him!"

Stephen privately thought it was much more likely that Peter Carver was simply a lousy gambler who didn't know how to get up from a poker table when he was losing. But this wasn't the time. He needed Christina on his side.

"The man who Peter owed the money to is dead. But the AF29 is still missing. As is Peter. There's an excellent chance he's still alive but Fortune and the others have hit a dead end. They need something to go on. Anything."

Christina sat for a long minute, chewing thoughtfully on her well-done steak. "There was a man who came by our flat a couple of times. A foreign gentleman. Very mannered. He and Peter talked. I just assumed he was somebody else Peter owed money to."

"You didn't catch this foreign gentleman's name?"

"No. It was an odd name, however…very odd…"

—∞∞∞—

The desk sergeant looked down from his imposing height at the smiling man standing before him. "That's an odd name. What'd you say it was again?"

"Sanusi. Lamido Sanusi."

"What is that? Eye-talian?"

"Actually, it's Gagrestrian. But that's not important." Sanusi held up a sparkling vial filled with a clear liquid that might have been water. But judging by the care with which this oddly named fellow held it, the sergeant figured it was anything but. "What is important is that I killed all those people in the bank this morning. And unless you and everybody in this building do exactly as I say, you will also be dead. I am Lamido Sanusi and I am the master of the Silent Death. Ignore me at my peril. Oh, bother!" Sanusi's handsome face broke out into a sudden, totally unexpected grin. "Apologies. I meant ignore me at your peril! You will have to excuse me. I'm still getting the hang of this."

"You're bluffing! You smash that thing in here and you're just as dead!"

"I smashed a vial just like this in the bank this morning and walked out smiling. You want to take the chance that I won't do the same right here and now? Lock up this building. Right now. Nobody leaves. And then I want to talk to the mayor."

—∞∞∞—

The radio in Fortune's car crackled for attention. He reached over and picked up the microphone. Tracy, sitting in the front seat half turned so that she could hear better. Ronald slowed down the car a bit.

"Fortune McCall here."

"McCall! It's Tate! There's a lunatic inside of Police Headquarters! He says he's got the killer virus. He's calling it the Silent Death and says he'll kill everybody in the building unless he talks to the mayor!"

"What have you done so far?"

"Cordoned off the building. Contacted the mayor. He'll be here in an hour."

"My people and I can be there in fifteen. Maybe we can do something before the mayor gets here."

"I damn sure hope you can. Because there's no way in hell I'm going to let Byles go into that building and that means a lot of good cops are going to die."

Police Headquarters resembled a castle set down right in the middle of the city. The largest, most imposing structure located across from historic Frasier Square, huge searchlights that lit up the building, staving off the quickly approaching night, now illuminated it. Tate insisted on a cordon three blocks back. In case a vial was dropped he wanted to make sure innocents were as far back as possible. He figured that three blocks away would be far enough. The infernal Silent Death dissipated quickly. The only ones in danger of being killed by the stuff would be the cops inside.

Fortune's car roared up the line of police cars blocking off Wallach Avenue. Fortune, Tracy, and Ronald climbed out, ran over to where Tate was waving them through the line of police officers.

"What would make this guy take an entire police station hostage?" Ronald wondered out loud. "He must know he can't get out of there alive!"

"Why not?" Fortune said. "He's been doing fine so far. Chief, I assume that there are ways into that building that do not appear on the official blueprints?" Fortune was familiar with the practice that most police departments had: they built their police stations with secret ways in and out just for situations such as this.

"You got that right. I was just waiting for you to get here. Figure I'd let you and your people take a crack at this guy first."

Tracy was holding a pair of full face gas masks in her hands. "I'm ready."

"Hey, where's mine?" Ronald demanded.

Fortune took his gas mask, shaking his head at the young man. "You're to stay outside with Chief Tate and wait for Eddie and Reggie. If Tracy and I do not make it, it'll be up to the three of you. Tell Eddie if Tracy and I do not come out by the time the mayor gets here, he's in charge." Fortune turned to Tate. "How do we get in?"

Tate took them to the side and quickly outlined the way in for Fortune and Tracy. For maximum security, those secret ways in and out were known only to high ranking officers, such as The Chief of Police, captains, and lieutenants.

Fortune and Tracy sprinted across the wide street to the rear of Police Headquarters. They were plainly illuminated in the small amount of time it took for them to do so but it was a chance they were willing to take.

———∞∞∞———

The elegant and palatial Amsterdam Hall had long been revered as one of the landmarks of Sovereign City. Part museum, part political meeting hall, part sanctuary, it rested on Sovereign City's ritzy Cutting Row like a large gray frog in a row of silver winged swans. The rest of the buildings along Cutting Row were bright and sparkling and looked almost new, so well were they maintained. Not so Amsterdam Hall which looked as if it had been constructed in a darker time for darker people.

Inside the main hall, servants dressed in Victorian era clothing moved among the two dozen men and women dining in the main hall. These men and women were clothed in modern day dress but they all had one thing in common: the masks they wore.

And such masks! Some were plain and simple, made of cloth or papier-mâché. Others were of silver, gold, bronze, iron, copper… some were ornate and baroque. Wonderfully detailed and worked into representation of their wearer's faces that were breathtaking in detail.

The Assembly of Masks gathered for dinner once a week and on those occasions when they were petitioned by someone eager to join their company. And on this night they had gathered to await word if their latest petitioner had accomplished the task before them.

At the head of the table, a portly man wearing a silver mask with onyx eyebrows and lips politely tapped his fork against his wine glass for attention. Twenty three masks turned toward his.

"As we await word on the success or failure of Mr. Sanusi, is there any other pressing business we should be discussing?"

A bronze mask decorated with peacock features nodded. "We should be lining up a candidate for the next mayoral elections. Mayor Byles is becoming most troublesome."

Silver Mask nodded in reply, as did all the other masks. The brilliant light of the chandeliers flashed from the jewels adorning their elaborate face wear.

A tall man entered the main hall. Licen had been the caretaker of Amsterdam Hall for twenty years now, inheriting the job from his uncle. He moved to the side of Silver Mask and whispered in his ear. Then as quietly as he came, he exited the room.

Silver Mask's laugh echoed around the room. "It could be that Mayor Byles will not be a problem for us very soon, my friends! Seems as if our Mr. Sanusi has gone us one better! He's not only holding Police Headquarters hostage, he's demanded to see the mayor as well!"

"Do you think Sanusi will do the same thing he did at the bank this morning? That he'll kill the mayor?" The speaker wore an elegant golden heron mask that sparkled with small diamonds.

Silver Mask raised his wine glass. "One can only hope, my dear. One can only hope!"

———— ∞∞∞ ————

Fortune and Tracy gained the inside of Police Headquarters thanks to a well hidden tunnel, the entrance of which had been cleverly disguised as a storm drain. The tunnel took them inside the imposing building and they ended up in the first floor office of the Police Commissioner, coming out of the fireplace. Despite the huge, imposing size of the fireplace, it swung open easily from the inside, so well designed were the pivots.

Tracy and Fortune slipped inside the semi-darkened office. "Where is everybody?" She wondered aloud in a soft voice.

"Let us split up. We-"

"No," Tracy said in a voice that brooked no argument. "There is no way I'm letting you out of my sight. Do you expect me to let you die and not die with you? Your mother and father would sell me to the Costinagi if I came back to them with a sad story of how you died heroically."

"Hm. You have a point. Mother would especially take umbrage. Very well. Come with me."

Tracy thrust a gas mask into his hand. Fortune threw his fedora on the desk and motioned for her to follow him.

Sanusi had gathered everybody in the building into the first floor auditorium. Sanusi had been smart enough to release the prisoners secured in the basement holding cells and arm them. So he now had fully a dozen desperate cohorts holding guns on the fifty police officers sitting in the front rows of the auditorium. There was no chance that the officers could fight back without getting cut down by the handguns and rifles in the hands of the criminals.

From outside, the amplified voice of Chief Tate boomed through the hand held cone of a metal megaphone. "This is Chief of Police Tate! I'm authorized to negotiate for the release of the hostages!"

Of course there was no negotiation planned. Tate's only purpose was to keep Sanusi occupied.

He strolled to the window, a vial in each hand. Supremely confident in his power and in his control of the situation, he waggled one vial out the window. "You'd do better to go get the mayor and send him in here and stop wasting time, Chief. I'm getting impatient."

"What do you want?"

"I want the mayor! And I want him here right soon! Stop stalling, Chief!"

Fortune and Tracy stayed close to the floor as they took up positions on either side of the main auditorium doors. "You figure out a way we're going to get inside?" Tracy wanted to know.

"I'm still working on that. We have to cause some sort of diversion."

"What about those vials? If he drops one-"

"He's bluffing. Those are not the vials with The Silent Death."

"How do you know?"

"Do you see him with a gas mask?"

"Maybe he's an out and out lunatic who doesn't care?"

Fortune handed Tracy two fat black canisters. "We must depend on speed and accuracy. Give me two minutes, then throw these inside."

"Wait! Where are you going?"

In answer, Fortune handed Tracy an item that made her grin. "Gotcha."

Outside on the street, Regina, Ronald, and Eddie were desperate to know what was going on inside and the seeming lack of action on the part of Chief Tate was even more frustrating.

"Aren't you going to do anything?" Regina demanded. "Or are you just going to stand there playing pocket pool?"

"Don't you think I want to?" Eddie replied glumly.

"So why don't you?"

"Because despite what Fortune said, I'm actually not the guy in charge. He is." Eddie pointed at Chief Tate. "Soon as we got here, Tate pulled me to the side and let me know in no uncertain terms that the mayor had given him orders to work with Fortune but he had no such orders to work with me. So I was to stand to the side, stay out of the way, and he wouldn't jail me for interfering with a police action."

"And you're just going to leave it at that?"

"What else do you expect me to do? There's a lunatic in there with the power to kill everybody in that building. We go off on our own hook and we may make the situation worse. Let's just hunker down and hope Fortune and Tracy can pull it off."

Tracy's entire body quivered with excitement as all the lights in the building suddenly went dark. Fortune had made his way to the basement and killed all the lights. Immediately the cops held hostage exploded into action, helped by surprise and the illumination from outside. They leaped upon the prisoners holding the weapons. The auditorium soon filled with curses, the sounds of fists smacking against flesh, the flashes from gun muzzles as weapons were discharged.

Tracy pitched the two black canisters inside and the tear gas quickly spread through the auditorium, adding to the general mayhem. She leaped over bodies rolling around on the floor, locked in battle. More shots filled the huge auditorium.

Thanks to the goggles Fortune had given her, she could see in the darkness. The goggles she wore amplified whatever available light there was and enabled her to avoid running into anybody as she made a beeline straight at Lamido Sanusi, who was himself doing a pretty good job of running for the stage.

Where are the vials? Tracy wondered. She didn't dare peg a shot at Sanusi lest he drop one. Even though Fortune didn't think he had The Silent Death, Tracy took no chances and held a gas mask in one hand, ready to slap it to her face if she saw Sanusi drop a vial.

He scrambled onto the stage and Tracy launched her pint-sized body in a desperate leap, tackling Sanusi and bringing him crashing down to the hardwood floor of the stage.

He pulled a leg back and pistoned it out, brutally smashing Tracy in the jaw. She rolled away, her goggles flying off her face, the gas mask dropping from her hand.

Sanusi scrambled to his feet, dramatically raised a vial while shouting, "Get back or everybody dies!"

From off to the right, Fortune's cultured, sardonic voice said, "Oh, do stop with the theatrics, please." He emerged from the side of the stage, racing right at Sanusi who dropped into the Third Defensive Stance of The Third Level of Llap-Goch. Fortune's estimation of his foe went up a notch. There were maybe only twenty-one people in the world advanced enough to get to the third level. Fortunately he was also one of those twenty-one.

Their arms and legs became a blur of strikes, kicks, and defensive blocks as they engaged each other, testing each other's strengths. Fortune stepped back, whipped off his fedora and flung it in Sanusi's face.

Sanusi slapped it away but that was more than enough time for Fortune to sweep his legs out from under him. Sanusi once again hit the floor but as he did so, he flung the two vials of The Silent Death into the air.

Tracy rolled underneath one vial, caught it in both hands. But the other went wildly wild and free, tumbling over and over in the air until it smashed on the floor.

Tracy instinctively held her breath but Sanusi seemed unworried at all and in fact was grinning as if he'd just told the world's funniest dirty joke. Fortune reached down and with both gloved hands, yanked Sanusi to his feet. "That's not The Silent Death, is it?"

What? Did you honestly think I would take a chance on it killing me?" Sanusi's cackling laughter was somehow off, as if he were laughing because he thought he should be laughing, not because he genuinely thought the situation funny. "No, I've got too much to do and too much fun to have with Sovereign City, Mr. McCall. It is Fortune McCall I'm addressing, isn't it?"

"It is."

"A pleasure, sir."

"Hope you continue to feel that way when you're sitting in Mr. Sparky preparing to ride the lightning." Fortune replied grimly. "You have been a busy lunatic today, sir. You've killed a lot of people that did you no harm."

"But not as many as I'm going to kill."

The lights came back on and there was something profoundly disturbing in Sanusi's eyes. Something Fortune had seen before but he could not say where or when.

Tracy sheepishly got to her feet. "You could have told me before I made a fool out of myself, y'know."

"But I did tell you," Fortune said. "Get my hat, will you?" He turned back to Sanusi. "Where is The Silent Death?"

"Oh, some friends of mine are holding it for me. I have plans for it, I assure you."

Fortune's hands tightened on the lapels of Lamido Sanusi's suit but there was nothing else he could do because Chief Tate, at the head of an army of police as well as Regina, Eddie, and Ronald rushed into the auditorium.

Across town, a basement door opened quietly. Peter Carver sat still tied in the chair. He'd passed out hours ago from dehydration and sheer exhaustion. On the table near him sat the satchel containing the vials of The Silent Death.

Licen, the caretaker of Amsterdam Hall entered the basement. He stood looking at the immobile form of Peter Carver for maybe a minute. He took a knife from his pants pocket. It was the work of a few minutes to cut the bonds holding Carver to the chair. As easily as if Carver weighed no more than a straw, Licen slung Carver over his shoulder.

Licen picked up the satchel full of death and left the basement.

———— ⊗∞⊗ ————

"So what's going to happen to this Sanusi guy?"
The question came from Pasquale Zollo. He, along with the others were taking dinner in the Classroom while Fortune, Ronald, Tracy, Regina, and Eddie brought him and Stephen up to speed on the day's events.

Fortune swallowed a mouthful of Caprese salad and said, "Chief Tate wants to keep him here in Sovereign City until The Silent Death is recovered. Sanusi himself has not said a word since he was taken into custody."

"Give him to me," Pasquale offered. "Leave me alone with him for an hour and I guarantee I'll find out where it is."

"It may come to that," Fortune said. "That cursed Silent Death is too dangerous to leave out there." He interlaced his long fingers. "I can't help but think that there is something unnatural behind Sanusi's actions. They made no sense but yet, there's some purpose behind everything he did, no matter how irrational."

"On the positive side, Dr. Carver was able to create an antidote of sorts to The Silent Death," Stephen said. "The drawback is that it's only effective for twenty-four hours. Which means that you have to take it before you're exposed to the stuff."

"So if you're not exposed to The Silent Death that means you've wasted a dose, right?" Regina said.

Stephen nodded in affirmation. "And if that happens it's another twenty-four hours before you can take another injection of the antidote. The antidote itself is so powerful that taking too much of it will kill you just as dead as The Silent Death."

"Speaking of our Dr. Carver," Fortune said with a smile. "Did you arrange her trip?"

Stephen smiled back. "Sure did, Fortune…she should be arriving there in three days…"

———— ⊗∞⊗ ————

Three Days Later
The North African country of Khusra

Dr. Christina Carver opened her eyes slowly. She had no idea where she was or what had happened. The last thing she remembered was being aboard Fortune McCall's gambling ship, talking with Mr. Lapinsky. Then she finished her work on the antidote and Mr. Lapinsky took her to a stateroom to get some much needed sleep. And now she was…where?

The room she was in was cool and white. The bed quite large and comfortable. She lay in the middle and it was big enough that two adults could have lain on either side of her without touching her. She looked down at her clothing. It had been changed. She now wore an ankle length black robe with a heavily embroidered front. Christina slid off the bed and moved through the wonderfully decorated room. She burst out onto the balcony and looked in amazement at what lay before her.

Whatever city she was in, in was not an American city. The architecture was plainly that of a foreign country. She was no expert in architecture but if one had been there with her they would have informed her that what she was looking at was reminiscent of Medieval Ethiopia. And it was hot. In fact, it was a familiar heat. In her internship she'd done some work in East Africa. That was the same kind of heat. Nowhere else on Earth but Africa had that quality of heat.

Christina heard someone behind her. She whirled to see an elegant, white haired black woman walking toward her. The woman walked as if the floor beneath her feet was of solid gold. Her entire bearing was that of regal serenity. And even though Christina was near frantic with hysteria, the white-haired woman's smile and demeanor let Christina know that she had nothing to fear from her.

"Who are you? Where am I? I demand to know why I was brought here!"

"Fortune McCall has requested that you be a guest here. You are in Mahaiso, the capital city of Khusra."

"And where the hell is Khusra?"

"North Africa."

"I demand you send me back to the United States at once!"

The white-haired woman walked closer. "Not until we have spoken. Fortune McCall has said that you must understand who he is. And more importantly what he is before you return to Sovereign City…"

The MAGIC of MADNESS

THE MAGIC OF MADNESS

───❀❀❀───

The Croxton Opera House seemed to throb and thrum with the thunderous applause of the audience within. Filled to capacity, two thousand pairs of hands clapped wildly for nearly two minutes. For the past hour, they had been thrilled by the illusions of Benjamin and Penelope Lash, magicians extraordinaire.

And Fortune McCall certainly was enthralled. He was on his feet, shouting 'Bravo!' as enthusiastically as he clapped.

Tracy Scott yanked on the tail of his tuxedo. "Sit down, will you? You're making a spectacle of yourself."

"Cease that at once," Fortune chided. But he did resume his seat. "I paid for this private box. Therefore I will continue to conduct myself as I please. And if I'm enjoying the performance-"

"I know what you're enjoying," Tracy muttered. "You haven't taken your eyes off of her since she hit the stage."

The 'her' Tracy referred to was the undeniably gorgeous Penelope Lash. She stood next to her husband, holding his hand and bowing. Benjamin Lash was golden haired and fair skinned. Penelope was dark haired, tanned an even golden brown that complimented the exotic cast of her face. Depending on how she held her face and the way the light struck it, she looked Asian one way, Egyptian another and even African another way. Both of them looked absolutely elegant. He in his midnight black tuxedo and she in her matching Bellucci sheath dress.

"I wager she has cool grey eyes," Fortune sighed.

"I wager her husband will make a good try at beating all the black off you if you make goo-goo eyes at his wife," Tracy said sharply.

"So I cannot appreciate a beautiful woman without lusting after her? Is that what you are saying?"

"I'm just saying-"Tracy broke off as Benjamin Lash spoke. His assistants wheeled a clear glass box the size of a steamer trunk onto the stage as he did so. Penelope stepped back and let her husband have the stage.

"Thank you, ladies and gentlemen. Thank you! My wife and I have been pleased and proud to entertain you this evening. But we have one final illusion to perform for you. And I can assure you that we truly have saved the best for last!"

Benjamin Lash indicated the glass box, which had been filled with water prior to being brought on stage. "This is an illusion that caused the death of the legendary Great Reddick in Germany! It is danger at the utmost level and if my beautiful wife Penelope and I have our concentration broken in the slightest, it could mean our deaths! That is why I must beg for complete and total silence during this illusion!"

Benjamin Lash stripped off his tuxedo jacket and pants, which were breakaways designed and sewn by his own hand. He kicked off his shoes and removed his socks, revealing a one piece red bathing suit he had been wearing underneath. His assistants stood nearby with an assortment of shackles. The orchestra played very softly as Penelope Lash spoke in a surprising husky voice:

"The box you see before you was constructed of Indestructo safety glass, manufactured by British Indestructo Glass, Ltd. The glass is two inches thick and cannot be broken by any means. I myself have watched my husband hit it with a ten pound sledgehammer to no effect."

"Let's see it for ourselves!" someone in the audience shouted.

Fortune smiled at Tracy. "A plant in the audience placed there by the Lashes themselves, no doubt."

"How do you know that?"

"I know something of the art of illusion."

Tracy sighed. "Of course you do."

An assistant bulging with muscles walked from offstage with a ten pound sledgehammer in his ham-sized hands. He planted his feet, brought the sledgehammer up, around, and down in a tremendous arc to impact upon the lid of the glass box. It did no damage whatsoever. A ripple of amazement went around the opera house.

Penelope resumed her speech. "As you can see, the box is impervious. My husband is being secured with handcuffs and leg irons. He will be placed inside the box, which will be padlocked shut. Once he is locked in there, no power on earth can get him out. My husband can hold his breath for an impressive amount of time, three minutes exactly. He has that long to extricate himself from his bonds and get out of the box. Can he do it? We will see."

Penelope walked over to where her husband stood and gave him a loving kiss. Huge manacles with chain links as thick as a big man's thumb bound his legs. Handcuffs encircled his wrists. He was picked up by two of his strongest male assistants and placed inside the box. The lid was then closed and padlocked shut. The assistants easily hoisted Penelope up on top of the box where she stood in plain sight, illuminated by the bright stage lights.

The audience sat in total silence, holding their collective breath as they watched Benjamin Lash inside the water filled box, struggling with his bonds. Slowly a black curtain was lowered, barely big enough to hide the box and Penelope from the sight of the audience.

Penelope's voice burst from behind the curtain. "One!"

The audience gasped.

Once more her voice rang out. "Two!"

And then, incredibly, Benjamin's voice called out, "Three!"

The curtain was dropped. Benjamin Lash now stood on top of the box, once more in his tuxedo and without so much as a drop of water on him! And within the water filled box the audience could plainly see that Penelope Lash was now within! She was manacled in the same fashion her husband had been and now it was she who wore the red one-piece bathing suit!

It was said the next day that the applause sounded like cannon fire, so loud was it. Benjamin nimbly hopped down from the box and turned to one of his assistants for the key to the padlock securing the lid. He put the key in the lock and turned.

Even from the private box, Fortune could tell that something had gone wrong. Benjamin twisted the key again and again but the padlock would not open.

Inside the water-filled box, Penelope's efforts to escape became more vigorous, more panicked. Benjamin frantically waved for his assistant with the sledgehammer to come back on stage with the tool. The big man did so and once again swung the hammer. It impacted on the side of the box with no effect whatsoever.

"Get her out!" a woman shrilly screamed. "Oh, dear God, get her out!"

Men wildly leaped out their seats, charging for the stairs up to the stage. Fortune himself was heading out of the box. "Tracy, did you bring lock picks? Maybe I can-"

That was when the lights went out and the opera house was plunged into total darkness! Men cursed, women screamed, and Benjamin's voice rang out, pleading for calm.

That was when the lights came back on!

And from the rear of the theater, a husky voice called, "I'm right here, darling! And I'm okay!" And yes, it was Penelope Lash who stood there, dripping wet but free of her manacles, waving gaily. And if the applause before had sounded like cannon fire, then this storm of applause that now raised the roof of the Croxton Opera House had to be likened to a volcano erupting.

⌘

Thirty minutes later, Fortune McCall knocked on the door of the suite of dressing rooms utilized by the Lashes. The door was opened by Benjamin himself, who waved Fortune and Tracy inside. "Come in, come in! Please!"

The dressing room looked more like a hotel suite, a testament to the reputation of The Croxton. Benjamin had taken off his tuxedo jacket and he steered Fortune and Tracy to comfortable chairs. He held one of Fortune's cards in his hand. "Well, you could have knocked me over with a feather when the usher brought me your card, Mr. McCall!"

"Why is that, sir?"

"I had tried to see you when you were in London a year or so ago. I had heard from other illusionists that you had studied briefly under Fettes The Fantastic in Edinburg   But by the time I could get word to you, you had lifted anchor and sailed away."

"My apologies, sir. One of the advantages of living on a ship is that when I get bored with the view I can simply go to another port. But it does make it disadvantageous for others at times."

Benjamin whirled around just as Penelope entered the room and said merrily, "Ah, there is my precious jewel! Penelope, may I introduce Mr. Fortune McCall and his associate, Miss Tracy Scott."

Close up, Penelope was even more breathtaking in her loveliness. There was something almost too perfect about the flawless beauty of her face. She offered her hand to be kissed, which Fortune did while hiding his surprise. White women just didn't go around offering their hands to be kissed by black men, especially when their husbands were standing right there. Which led Fortune to think that his initial impression that Penelope Lash was of biracial ancestry was correct.

"My husband and I heard a great deal about you in London, Mr. McCall."

"So he tells me, Mrs. Lash. I am most apologetic that I was called away on urgent business before we could meet. And may I say that your performance tonight was simply incredible. Especially the final illusion. I have seen it performed before, but never with the added touch of the person in the box appearing at the rear of the auditorium."

Benjamin and Penelope grinned like a couple of schoolkids who had just put one over on the teacher. "We are the only stage magicians to do that!" Benjamin said, obviously proud of that fact. "There are magicians the world over who would give their right leg to know how it is done."

"I don't suppose I could persuade you to tell me how you did it for $10,000?" Fortune said with a wicked grin.

"I wouldn't tell you for $100,000, Mr. McCall," Benjamin laughed.

Fortune joined him in laughter. Of course Benjamin wouldn't tell him. That illusion was worth much, much more. Eventually he would pass on the secret to another magician, most likely one he would train himself. But in the meantime, the money he would make from performing that illusion around the world would make $10,000 look like pocket change.

"The hour grows late and I still have much to do before I can retire," Fortune said. "But I insist that you both come aboard The Heart of Fortune tomorrow for lunch. Or perhaps dinner if you do not have an evening performance?"

"In fact, we don't." Penelope turned to her husband. "Oh, do let us go, Ben! I've heard so much about Mr. McCall's ship!"

Benjamin smiled and nodded. "Would eight o'clock be fine?"

"Why not come a little earlier than that? Say around six? This way I can give you and Mrs. Lash a proper tour of my pride and joy. And after dinner you can gamble to your heart's content. As my guests, of course. In fact, bring a change of clothing so that you can stay overnight."

"We'd be delighted to do so, Mr. McCall," Benjamin shook hands with Fortune. After passing a few more pleasantries with the Lashes, Fortune and Tracy left the dressing room and walked through the narrow backstage corridors.

Fortune gave Tracy a superior smile as he said, "By the way, did you notice that I was right?"

Tracy frowned slightly. "About what?" She replied, adjusting her fox stole around her shoulders.

"She does have cool gray eyes."

⎯⎯⎯⎯⎯⎯

Benjamin unlocked the door of their suite and held it open for Penelope. They were staying in the Dante Suite at the Palace Hotel. Consisting of three bedrooms, a grand salon and a dining room, the ceilings were nearly fifteen feet high. Windows overlooked the nighttime splendor of Sovereign City.

"Would you like a nightcap, darling?" Benjamin asked as he helped his wife off with her wrap.

"I'd much rather we sit down and talk, Benjamin."

"We can sit and talk, surely. You go on and make yourself comfortable. I'll get the drinks. Did you hear that applause tonight? They'll remember us for years!"

"You act as we're going to retire tomorrow."

Benjamin mixed Manhattans for both of them as he answered her. "There's no retirement fund for magicians, Penelope. We need to start looking out for ourselves in that regard. I'm thinking about our old age."

"Benjamin, are you going to be honest with me about what's going on with you?"

Benjamin walked over to the Louis XV style couch his wife sat on and handed a cocktail glass to her. His voice was light and playful but his eyes held shadows within as he said, "I'm sure I don't know what you mean, darling."

"Benjamin, I'm not stupid. You changed our booking dates so that we we're here playing Sovereign City a whole six months ahead of schedule. Why?"

"I-" hearing a knock at the door, Benjamin broke off and put down his glass on a nearby table. "That must be room service with our late dinner. Let me take care of this as quickly as possible and then we can continue our talk."

Penelope plainly didn't like being interrupted but she also couldn't deny that she was famished and dinner would be welcome. She heard Benjamin open the door and then she heard something that made her whirl around in surprise. What she had heard was her husband gasp in pain.

The men pushing into the room were Oriental, all dressed in midnight black suits and fedoras. One man had Benjamin in what appeared to be an excruciatingly painful arm lock, judging by the look on his face. Five men in all. One leveled a long barreled revolver at Penelope, motioning for her to sit down and be quiet, while the others spread out to search the suite. They returned in less than a minute, conveying the information that they were alone.

The man with the gun said to Penelope, "Our business is with your husband. We are men and we deal with men as men. If you behave yourself and stay in a woman's place, you will not be harmed, molested, or killed. I do not repeat myself." The man with the gun, obviously the leader now spoke to Benjamin, "Where is our package?"

"Let Penelope go first! She's got nothing to do with this!"

The leader nodded and the sound of Benjamin's left pinky being broken made Penelope cry out in horror. "Bastards! Leave him alone!"

The leader stepped forward and swung his left arm briskly, taking Penelope across the mouth in a slap hard enough to cause pain and make his intention clear but not hard enough to draw blood. He returned to Benjamin. "I remind you that you have nine remaining unbroken fingers. Once we have broken them we can move on to your arms, legs, and twenty four ribs. I ask again: where is our package?"

Penelope snarled, "We don't have anything of yours! Leave us alone!"

"Your husband does. We have an agreement he has broken. He knows what we are talking about."

Penelope looked at Benjamin. His face had gone gray from shock and thickly coated with sweat. "Benjamin…oh, Benjamin…what have you gotten yourself into?"

The man who had broken Benjamin's finger let him go and Benjamin dropped to the floor like a pig carcass. "Maybe we should work on the woman," he suggested.

The leader frowned. "Did you not hear me give my word to the woman she would not be harmed? I-"

Penelope wasn't waiting around for the leader to be persuaded to change his mind regarding her personal safety. There was no point making a try for the door leading out to the corridor. She'd never make it. And one of the Orientals stood in front of the bedroom door. She abandoned the idea of running in there, closing and locking the door and calling for help from the phone within.

Penelope looked at the half open double doors leading out to the balcony. Well, it wasn't ideal, but it was her only chance.

Pushing herself off the couch, Penelope ran to the balcony with the grace of a gazelle, even in the high heels she wore. She lifted up her dress so that she would not stumble on the hem. Behind her, the Orientals shouted. She caught them totally by surprise as they had not expected her to make a run for the balcony. And that surprise gained her a few precious seconds. Penelope threw a last word of encouragement over her shoulder. "Stay brave, darling! I'll come back with help!"

Her shoulder struck the half open doors, forcing them to fly apart. Penelope took two long steps and then leaped off the balcony!

The leader was no more than three heartbeats behind her. He looked over the railing, expecting to see the woman's body plummeting to the street far below. His eyes opened wide in total and utter astonishment.

Penelope Lash was nowhere in sight!

The Dante Suite occupied the fifteenth floor of The Palace Hotel. There were flagpoles decorating the front of the hotel but she was not hanging from any of them and there was nothing else the woman could have grabbed onto to brake her fall. Incredible as it seemed, Penelope Lash jumped off the balcony and...disappeared.

The leader's men were shouting questions at him. He figured it was best not to divulge the truth and turned back to the brightly lit room. "She was weak and foolish like all women and leaped to her death! She is not our concern!"

Despite his pain, Benjamin managed a laugh that had a tinge of hysteria in it. "Tell them the truth if you have the guts! She's gone, isn't she?" Benjamin laughed louder. "You do know she's a magician, right?"

The leader cracked the long barrel of his gun against the side of

Benjamin's head, knocking him out. He turned to silence the excited demands of his men as they wanted to know what Benjamin meant.

"Be silent! I said the woman is dead! Pick this man up and bring him. We still must find the location of our merchandise!"

———∝∞∞———

Fortune McCall walked onto the top deck of The Heart of Fortune which were his own personal living quarters and breathed in the fresh air. After being inside the smoky confines of his casino for several hours, it was more than a blessing to be able to enjoy the breeze. Dawn smudged the horizon and Fortune saw with pleasure that his dinner had already been placed on the table and his manservant Obarr stood nearby waiting to serve him.

Most people in Sovereign City were sitting down to breakfast but for Fortune, dinner was breakfast. He was a night person, always had been ever since childhood. He would pretend to go to sleep when tucked in by his mother or one of the many servants in the service of his father. But then he would climb out of bed once the door was closed and stay up reading. He loved the stories of The Three Musketeers, Robin Hood, Cyrano, and other adventurers and dreamed of the day when he would be old enough to travel the world and have adventures of his own.

"Dreams do come true, Obarr. Never let anybody tell you different," Fortune said cheerfully as he sat down.

"If you say so, sir." Obarr replied dourly as he served coffee. Obarr had been in Fortune's service ever since Fortune was five years old and in all that time, Fortune could not recall the man having another expression on his long, basset hound face other than the one he had now. He looked like a man who's been told he's got thirty days to live on the twenty-ninth day. He also never seemed to age. To Fortune he looked exactly the same now as he did the day they met.

Eddie Padilla came up the stairs, pausing himself to enjoy the breeze. "Man, that feels good." He walked over to the table, a number of papers in his hand.

"Coffee, Mr. Padilla?" Obarr asked.

"Sure. Thanks a lot. How'd last night go?" This last bit was directed at Fortune. All of his friends helped him run and operate the floating gambling casino that was the Heart of Fortune on a rotating schedule. Fortune was there every night because he enjoyed it so much but not all of his friends shared his love of staying up all night every night. Last night had been Eddie's night off. And in any case, in Eddie's capacity as Fortune's lawyer it was more necessary that he be up during the day than some of the others since he had Fortune's proxy to act in his name when Fortune was asleep or otherwise occupied.

"Good, good," Fortune replied, forking down medium rare rib eye steak. "The take for last night was outstanding. We're doing well here in Sovereign."

"This would be a good time to ask for a raise, then." Eddie rattled the papers in his hand. "As per the instructions you slipped under my door, I got on the radiophone and dug up the info you wanted."

"Ah! Let me see, let me see!" Fortune wiped his hands on the silk napkin in his lap and shuffled through the papers, reading the highlights of what he wanted to know. He looked up at Eddie. "She's Hawaiian and Negro?"

Eddie nodded. "More than that...your Mrs. Lash is rumored to be related to Hawaiian royalty. Why such an interest in this woman? We got a caper going?"

"No. I simply wanted to know more about the woman, is all."

"Including that she's married. You do know that, don't you?"

Fortune looked up, irritated. "You must have talked to Tracy."

"I might."

"I assure you that my interest in this woman stems from purely professional motives. I'm impressed by her talent and the notoriety she has achieved in a profession dominated by men."

"That's the exact same thing you said about the French ambassador's wife in Madagascar. I do not intend to go through that kind of circus again. I mean it, Fortune."

"Edward, I-"

"The choice appears to have been taken out of our hands."

Fortune and Eddie turned toward the sound of Tracy's voice. She stood there, a grim expression on her elfin face. Shivering next to her was the very wet and very frightened looking Penelope Lash, wrapped in a thick blanket, water puddling at her feet. She fixed Fortune with grey eyes that were no longer cool.

"Mr. McCall. I badly need your assistance. I think my husband has either been killed or will be soon. Unless you can help me."

—∞∞∞—

Fortune McCall stepped off the service elevator onto the fifteenth floor of The Palace Hotel, followed by Tracy, Eddie, and Penelope Lash, who was now dressed more appropriately, thanks to Regina Mallory's wardrobe. The three of them quietly walked to the bend in the hallway and Fortune stealthily looked around the corner. The hallway was full of policemen and reporters. Fortune grinned at the others. "Sometimes there are definite advantages to not being allowed to ride in the main elevators." Fortune gestured at a nearby service closet. Tracy took Penelope by the elbow and the two women entered, Penelope with extreme reluctance. "I want to go with you! I want to find out what's happened to my husband!"

Fortune whispered urgently, "You've indicated that you think your husband might be involved in some illegal activity. Now if you fall into the hands of the authorities, you will be detained and asked all sorts of embarrassing questions you cannot answer. Do you want that or do you want to be free to help me find out what's become of him?"

Penelope bit her lower lip in a manner that Fortune found quite fetching. "Very well," she said. "But I want to know everything you find out!"

"My word on it. Now get in there and be still."

Fortune and Eddie strolled down the hall until reaching the mob of police and reporters. "Hey, it's Fortune McCall!' one of the reporters yelled. "You working this case, Fortune?"

Fortune held up gray gloved hands. "I don't even know if there is a case here, boys. I just came by to see the Lashes. They're friends of mine, don't you know. What's the rumpus?"

From inside the suite a booming voice emerged, "Is that Fortune McCall out there? Let him in!"

Fortune and Eddie went on into the suite. It was Chief of Police Tate who had done the bellowing. He stood with another man. This man towered over the other three due to his height of 6' 4". But he appeared to be even taller due to his standing so ramrod straight it seemed as if it had to be painful to maintain such an upright carriage. He dressed in a severe black business suit with his only concession to style being the red silk Kentucky tie and the broad brimmed hat held in one sinewy hand.

The face that turned to regard Fortune might as well have been carved out of sun-darkened wood. High cheekbones, a mustache and hair trimmed with such severe precision that it might have been done by a machine instead of a human barber. Eyes the color of flint with no emotion in them whatsoever flickered briefly over Eddie and turned back to Fortune. "McCall," he said in a deep and resonant voice.

Fortune took off his storm cloud gray fedora and nodded back. "Captain. I don't believe you know my associate. Edward Padilla, Captain John Lawman."

Captain John Lawman shook Eddie's hand but his eyes never left Fortune. "You been asked by the mayor to work this case, McCall?"

"I didn't even know there was a case to be worked, Captain."

Chief Tate spoke up. "That stage magician Ben Lash and his wife are staying here, McCall. A gang of celestials busted into the joint last night, dragged out the husband at gunpoint. Couple of the bellboys tried to stop them coming in and out. They got cracked skulls for their pains."

"But the wife doesn't appear to be here and according to a dozen witnesses she wasn't taken with her husband..." Captain John Lawman's eyes were boring into Fortune's. "Exactly why are you here, McCall?"

"I met the Lashes backstage last night after their performance. I was supposed to meet them here for breakfast and then escort them back to my ship where they were to be my guests for the rest of the day."

"Then you haven't seen the wife?"

"Should I have?"

Captain Lawman's eyes narrowed slightly. "Did some checking on you when you first showed up in Sovereign. Some interesting facts in your history, McCall. Including that you seem to have a thing for other men's wives." Then he abruptly placed his hat on his head of silver-gray hair. "With your permission, Chief Tate, I'll be about my business, see if I can get a lead on the wife."

Chief Tate touched two fingers to the stingy brim of his cap. "Certainly, Captain. You'll be in touch?"

"When I have something to tell you." Captain Lawman turned those eyes back on Fortune. "Seeing as how the Lashes are such 'good friends' of yours, McCall, I 'spect you'll be rooting 'round in this?"

"I would not dream of impeding your investigations, Captain."

Captain Lawman emitted a sound that might have been a grunt of satisfaction and then he was gone.

Chief Tate turned back to Fortune and Eddie. "Not much you can do here, McCall."

"Do you think this is a kidnapping, Chief?"

"McCall, I dunno what this is. Nothing's been stolen. There's a wad of bills on the nightstand in the bedroom. I reckon that's the husband's roll. The wife's jewelry is on the makeup table. Far as we can tell, nothing's been stolen. Of course, we'd need the wife or the husband to verify that but my guess is that robbery had nothing to do with this. The celestials wanted the husband right enough and they got him."

"Suppose I look around for the wife myself?" Fortune asked with total innocence in his voice. "While I'm sure Captain Lawman will find her, it certainly can't hurt for me to make some inquiries?"

Chief Tate shrugged. "I don't see what you can do that Captain Lawman can't. But what the hell...long as you don't step on the Captain's toes, go on ahead."

Fortune bowed his head slightly and left the suite with Eddie. The reporters were thankfully gone, following after Captain Lawman and so the two men were able to walk back to the supply closet unmolested.

"Who's the gargoyle?" Eddie wanted to know.

"Captain Lawman? The story is he's a Texas Ranger who tracked his brother's killer to Sovereign City. He caught him, turned him over to the authorities here. Mayor Byles was impressed with him and the way he worked. So impressed he made Captain Lawman the same deal he made with me. He even gave the Captain his own precinct over in the Eighth Ward."

"He doesn't like you, does he?"

"Oh, you mean the way he acts? The Captain acts that way with everybody. Even Mayor Byles. One gets used to it after a while." Fortune frowned. "One day I must do something about that blatant lie going around having me chasing after married women."

Unseen by Fortune, Eddie rolled his eyes in exaggerated exasperation.

Upon hearing their voices, Penelope Lash burst from the closet. "Where's my husband? Is he all right? What did the police say?"

Fortune placed calming hands on her shoulders. "They don't know anything more than what you've already told us: your husband was abducted by a group of Oriental men. I saw no blood on the floor or the furniture so that most likely means that outside of the broken finger he was not injured further."

"But where is he? What could those men want with him?"

Tracy spoke up. "I say we get back to the ship and make our plans there. Anybody's likely to come along at any moment and once they see Mrs. Lash…"

Fortune nodded and motioned for them to board the service elevator.

———∞———

Back aboard The Heart of Fortune, Fortune McCall convened with the rest of his associates. Regina Mallory and Stephen Lapinsky joined Fortune, Tracy, and Eddie. Fortune's remaining two associates, Ronald Scocco and Pasquale Zollo, weren't present. Zollo was taking a week to visit his wife and children in the Italian town of Corleone. Zollo's family owned and operated several restaurants in the town and once a month, no matter where in the world he was, he flew home for a visit. He usually took Ronald with him. Having been abandoned by his parents as a child, Ronald immensely enjoyed the feeling of a huge family and Pasquale certainly had that.

"What is it with the women in Sovereign City?" Regina said to Stephen Lapinsky. He paused in the placing of tobacco in the bowl of his pipe. He gave her a puzzled look.

"What do you mean by that?"

"I mean that it seems as if ever since we've come to Sovereign City we've spent a considerable amount of time and effort chasing down lost or missing husbands. Can't these women hold onto their men?"

Stephen laughed softly. "I think it's a bit more complicated than that if the attention Fortune is giving Mrs. Lash is any indication."

Regina sniffed. "Don't think I haven't noticed. Remember the band leader's wife in New York?"

"Oh, yes. I do indeed."

Fortune rapped knuckles on the table for attention. "Here is the situation so far: Mrs. Lash's husband Benjamin was abducted this morning by a gang of armed Orientals. Mrs. Lash herself barely escaped. As yet, we don't know why he was kidnapped but Mrs. Lash thinks it has something to do with something illegal her husband might be involved in."

"Which explains her reluctance to go to the police," Eddie added. "I've offered my services as legal representative if she would go to the authorities but Mrs. Lash has refused."

"I want to find my husband before the police do! I'm sure that whatever it is, Benjamin was forced into it! He wouldn't do anything illegal unless he had been coerced in some way! Perhaps those men threatened to harm me if he didn't do what they said!'"

"Hold it just a minute, sister," Regina held up a hand. "You keep saying you think your husband is mixed up in something shady. Is he or isn't he?"

"I'm not sure. But for the past year Benjamin has been shifting around booking dates without consulting me or our business manager. He simply goes ahead and changes the dates with no warning whatsoever. He changed a date so that we would be here in Sovereign City, six months ahead of schedule."

"That isn't much to go on, Fortune," Regina said firmly. "I thought we were here in Sovereign to do some real good, not track down strayed husbands. Why not let the police handle this? We're busy people."

"Obviously you are not married," Penelope snapped, her gray eyes as frosty as her tone.

"If I were I'd do a much better job of keeping track of my husband than the women of this town."

"That's enough, Regina. Since you seem to have a problem with this caper, you can stay aboard The Heart and keep things running here. Since these men are Orientals, the logical place for us to start would be in Sovereign City's Chinatown district. Regular reports every hour and Regina, double the watch on the ship and if you haven't heard from either team for three hours-"

"I know. Come a'runnin' with a bunch of Otwani."

"Indeed."

———— ∞ ————

Like most major American cities and in fact, like most cities around the world, Sovereign City had a Chinatown. And like most Chinatowns Sovereign City's possessed a vibrant, fierce cultural identity that made one feel as if they had entered an entirely different world. Fortune and his associates left the cars they had used to get from the waterfront parked near the gloriously decorated paifang that was the entrance to Chinatown. Fortune issued swift instructions. "Mrs. Lash and Tracy, you'll come with me. We'll take the west side. Eddie, Stephen, you boys take the east side. Stop in at the Chinatown Businessmen's Association first and speak with them. You are both armed?"

Eddie and Stephen silently patted underneath their left armpits where they both had .38 revolvers snugly holstered. Fortune nodded.

"This is a fact finding mission. Ask questions, don't be afraid to spread money if necessary. We meet back here in two hours."

Fortune didn't have to ask Tracy if she was armed. Tracy was armed even when taking a bath or sleeping. Underneath his storm cloud gray duster, Fortune was armed with his habitual weapon of choice: a sawed off Browning A-5 pump shotgun. Despite his expertise with a staggering variety of exotic weaponry, Fortune was a notoriously terrible shot with handguns. With rifles and shotguns he was better than average, though.

"Where are we going?" Tracy asked, falling into step with Fortune.

"I thought we'd go see Mr. An."

Tracy shook her head. "You know he'll think you're coming for the ten large he owes you from two weeks ago."

"I will gladly tear up his marker in exchange for any information he can supply."

"Hey!" Penelope shouted. She had been trying to keep up with Fortune and Tracy, half trotting two or three steps behind them. "Where are we going? What are you doing? What has this to do with finding my husband?"

"My apologies, Mrs. Lash. I should be keeping you up to date at all times. We're here to find the men who kidnapped your husband."

"What makes you think they're here?"

"They were Orientals, Mrs. Lash. They would not have dreamed of going to such a well-known establishment as The Palace Hotel and kidnapping a white man in front of witnesses unless they had the blessing of some extraordinarily powerful people. Now, Stephen and Eddie are going to talk to the Chinese Businessmen's Association. That is the public face of Chinatown's ruling elite. We go to speak to one of the secret faces that also rules Chinatown."

"I see. You're a well-informed man, Mr. McCall."

They walked down tight, narrow streets as crooked as a spiral staircase after an earthquake. Here in Chinatown the street signs as well as signs above businesses and shops and restaurants were written in the native language and not English. Sovereign City's Chinatown held to its own identity with tenacity. They shortly arrived at their destination. Penelope looked up at the sign, frowning slightly.

"Sum Dum Goy Fortune Cookie Factory? Are you sure we're in the right place?"

"You read Cantonese?" Fortune asked.

"I know my way around a menu. Let's leave it at that," Penelope said. Tracy eyed her with a new respect as Fortune knocked on the door. A small square peephole opened and words exchanged between Fortune and the man behind the door in rapid and fluent Cantonese. The door opened and so Fortune, Tracy, and Penelope were ushered through the busy factory to the inner office of Mr. An. The man escorting them didn't seem pleased by their arrival and openly scowled as he opened the door to Mr. An's office.

He stood up as they entered his office. "Mr. McCall. You honor me by visiting my poor place of business. Please make yourselves comfortable while I have tea brought." Mr. An gestured at the man still waiting at the door, bidding him to bring tea. The man left slowly, softly closing the door.

Fortune took off his hat and bowed respectfully. "I beg you not to go to the trouble. We have come without warning or proper notice of intention to visit and so you should not feel obligated to extend us courtesy."

"Nonsense. I insist that you and the ladies be seated and partake of tea." Mr. An came from behind his desk. He gestured at comfortable leather chairs but nobody sat. His silky black hair hung down his back in an elegant, but businesslike style. Short, with a thin build he didn't seem very formidable at all. Looks were deceiving. In his younger days, Mr. An had been one of the most feared hatchet men in San Francisco's Chinatown before retiring from that life and moving to Sovereign City to start a new one. His considerable personal wealth as well as his reputation had assured him a position of influence and respect here. "I trust that each dawn has brought a day of success."

Fortune bowed again and replied, "and that each dusk an evening of contentment."

The obligatory pleasantries having been properly observed, the two men got down to business. "I trust this is not about the money I owe from the wonderful night I spent aboard your ship?" Mr. An's voice was pleasant enough but his eyes held a message that he was not one to have his word or his credit questioned.

"Of course not. The word of Mr. An is as reliable as the rising of the morning sun and twice as exalted. No, I come for another piece of business. In fact, if you can help me, I would be delighted to forget your debt."

"You are here about the white man kidnapped from the hotel this morning."

Fortune bowed again. "You are indeed a man of wisdom."

"Did you have my husband kidnapped?" Unable to contain herself any longer, Penelope shoved past Fortune. "Where is he? Is he here?"

Mr. An looked at Penelope as he might have looked at a puppy piddling on the floor. "This is the wife, I take it?"

Penelope whirled on Fortune. "Why aren't you making him talk? Why are you just standing there?"

"Easy, lady," Tracy laid hold of Penelope's elbow and yanked her from in between the two men. "Just stand here and keep your mouth shut."

"Why are you interested in this white man?" Mr. An asked Fortune with honest curiosity. "You and I are both pilgrims in this unholy land of greed and ignorance, forced to adopt the ways of barbarians to survive and thrive here. What concern is this man to you?"

"His wife asked me for help. I agreed to help her. She deserves to know what happened to her husband."

"Her husband's business is his own. If he did not see fit to tell her that business then perhaps it is best she does not know."

"Excuse me," Penelope stepped forward again, but this time her voice was quiet. "I apologize for the way I spoke before. Mr. An, are you married?"

Mr. An nodded. "I have two wives. One here and one in San Francisco. Between them they have blessed me with many strong sons and beautiful daughters."

"If something happened to you, wouldn't you want them to know? So that they could mourn you, if nothing else? Would you want them to live out the rest of their days with a big black hole of ignorance sucking away the sunlight of happy memories together?"

Mr. An sized up Penelope with new eyes. "I am not unmoved by your words. Please, sit." The three of them did so while Mr. An appeared to be wrestling with some inner conflict. He looked at Fortune. "You are a learned man. Therefore I will assume that you have heard of the Ui Kwoon Ah-How?"

Fortune replied, "A secret society of considerable power and influence, correct?"

Mr. An nodded. "It's unusual in the makeup of its membership. Any of Asian descent are welcome in its ranks. Chinese and Japanese willing serve in the Ui Kwoon Ah-How arm-in-arm with Koreans, Malayans, Mongols, Filipinos. It is totally unprecedented. But the master of the

Ui Kwoon Ah-How is a man who has somehow found the connecting thread to bind together so many and forge them into a single sword he intends to plunge into the heart of the world."

"Who is this master?"

"I dare not speak his name. I have said enough already to cause my death if it is ever known that I even dared to speak aloud the name of the Ui Kwoon Ah-How to outsiders. I will make a few phone calls and see what I can find out. And let me see what is keeping Wang with that tea."

Mr. An walked over to the door and opened it. Wang stood there. Obviously he had not gone to get the tea. His eyes glittered with fanatic hatred. With one swift motion, he withdrew a long knife from inside his left sleeve and plunged the bright blade into Mr. An's heart!

———— ∞∞∞ ————

"I've never been given the bum's rush so politely," Stephen Lapinsky said wryly as he lit his pipe. He and Eddie Padilla stood on the sidewalk outside the Chinatown Businessmen's Association headquarters. Their meeting with the half-dozen poker faced Businessmen's Executive Board had been excruciatingly short and to the point.

The Executive Board themselves had not spoken at all. They let their lawyer do that for them. A lawyer of considerable skill and reputation himself and unimpressed by Eddie's credentials. The lawyer suggested that since Mr. Padilla and Mr. Lapinsky were not representatives of the police then their request to ask questions had no validity. Eddie promptly replied he was representing Mrs. Lash and as her attorney, he did indeed have a valid right to ask questions.

The lawyer smiled generously, bowed and suggested that Mr. Padilla return with his client and then, with all parties present and all legal representation in place, proper questioning could be conducted.

"Didn't think you'd give up so easy, Eddie. I've seen you tongue dance around fancier suits than that one."

"Just the fact he was there told me something. You don't have your lawyer on standby unless you expect somebody with a badge or a warrant to come around answering questions. It's my guess the police have either been here or are on their way. In either case, those lads have pulled the wagons in a circle. We'll get nothing out of them."

"Next move?"

Eddie gestured at their parked car. "Let's check in with Regina, find out if Fortune's found anything."

Thanks to the radiophone, Eddie was talking to Regina in mere minutes. "Anything to report?" he asked while Stephen started up the car.

"Not a thing. All quiet out here. How'd you do?"

"Embarrassingly bad. Any word from His Highness?"

"Nope. You going to try and find him?"

"I've got a good idea of where he is. Mr. An owes him a lot of dough. Knowing Fortune, he'll try to exchange whatever dope Mr. An knows for the marker. Stephen and I'll head over to his joint."

"Good deal. Stay in touch."

—∞—

"**T**hus die all traitors!" Wang shrieked as he yanked the knife out of Mr. An's chest. The blade that had been so clean and bright just seconds ago was now red with blood from tip to hilt. A misty spray of arterial blood burst from the wound. Wang slammed the blade home a second time then turned and ran.

Fortune and Tracy plunged after him in hot pursuit. Tracy had a .45 automatic in one hand, angling for a shot but Fortune shouted, "No! I need him alive to question!"

"I can bring him down without killing him!"

"If you save your breath you can catch him instead!"

Wang sped through the crowded interior of the warehouse with confidence since he knew it far better than Fortune or Tracy who were forced to go around benches or machinery or piled boxes whereas Wang seemed to know hidden ways to actually go through. The workers in the warehouse shouted excited questions that were ignored by the pursuers and the pursued. The smoky interior of the warehouse didn't help either. Fortune and Tracy lost sight of their quarry.

"This way! Hurry! He went this way!" About nine or ten feet off to their left, Penelope Lash pointed at a branching hallway that slanted downward.

"How'd she get ahead of us so fast?" Tracy wondered aloud as she followed Fortune. But sure enough, they could see Wang running full speed down the slanting corridor.

"I'll go after him! Tracy, get back to the car with Miss Lash while I follow-"

"We're wasting time! He'll get away!" Penelope took off after Wang.

Over her shoulder as she followed Penelope, Tracy yelled at Fortune, "For once I agree with her!"

Fortune said nothing, simply followed. Indeed, there was no time to do anything else.

The pursuit ended at a huge wooden door Wang had shut behind him and they could hear bolts on the other side being thrown that locked it tight.

Fortune gave Tracy a simple order, "I wish to enter."

Tracy grinned, reached into a side pocket of her sheepskin aviator jacket and withdrew a hand grenade. She pulled the pin, rolled it on the floor toward the door. She ran back to where Fortune and Penelope took cover behind a stack of packing crates. The same time the grenade bumped against the door, it went off.

The orange red explosion illuminated the inside of the warehouse like a two-second dawn. The workers dashed out into the street, yelling for help or calling on the protection of their ancestors in a dozen different dialects.

Fortune used his fedora to wave dirt and dust away from his face. "Come!" he commanded and plunged through the space where the door had once been. The corridor continued onwards. Fortune and Tracy gave each other a look and saw in the eyes of the other the thrill of the adventure. Tracy grinned and hefted her .45 automatic. "Looks like we found a lot more than we bargained for, cousin."

"Indeed. We must proceed with caution but Mrs. Lash, you should-" Fortune's voice broke off as he looked around. "Tracy? Where did she go?"

Tracy's head swiveled back and forth in futile search of the elusive Penelope Lash. "Damn if I know. But I do know I wish she'd stop doing that. Gives me the creeps. We going to look for her?"

"No. Something tells me our mysterious Mrs. Lash is more adept at looking out for herself than we first supposed. Our task is to find that man. He killed Mr. An for a reason and I suspect it was to stop him from telling us more about the Ui Kwoon Ah-How. And besides,"

Fortune replaced his storm cloud gray fedora on his head and grinned at Tracy, "since he killed Mr. An, that man has now inherited his debt and I always get what is owed to me!"

———∞∞∞———

Stephen braked the car to a halt and looked out through the windshield in amazement. "What the hell?" he wondered out loud. He swapped a quick worried look with Eddie before they both climbed out.

The Sum Dum Goy Fortune Cookie Factory was cordoned off by half a dozen police cars. Smoke drifted from several broken windows. Barricades had been set up and a pair of burly officers waved at Stephen and Eddie as they approached.

"Dontcha see this street is off limits? Beat it before we run ya in."

"Hold on, officer. I know one of those men." Captain John Lawman strode forward, his eyes locked on Eddie. "You're McCall's man, aren't you? Who is this with you?"

"What's going on here, Captain? Trouble?"

"Suppose you answer my questions, first. What are you doing here?"

"Looking for a restaurant we were supposed to meet Mr. McCall at for a bite. You haven't seen him have you?"

Captain Lawman looked at Eddie as if trying to stare a hole in his skull. "You know full well McCall was here. I got that much from the description from a factory worker willing to talk. I also got Mr. An lying in his office with a knife in his chest. Didn't Mr. An owe McCall a lot of money?"

"You want to watch what you say, Captain." Eddie handed over his business card. "I'm Mr. McCall's legal representative as well as his friend and in both capacities I don't appreciate what you're implying."

"And besides, aren't we all on the same side?" Stephen put in. "Mayor Byles has the same arrangement with Mr. McCall that you have."

"Add to that the fact that Mr. McCall is a respected businessman and is rapidly establishing himself as a vital and enriching citizen of Sovereign City." Eddie finished.

"Fortune McCall is a gambling two-bit hustler who got lucky with that arrangement. If it wasn't for that deal I'd have run McCall and the whole lot of you out of Sovereign and blown up that cursed ship."

"Again, I advise you to cease your groundless allegations against Mr. McCall."

"McCall thinks that just because he provides a place for overgrown children to waste their money he's protected from the law. He thinks just because he does the mayor a couple of favors he can do whatever he likes."

"Funny, Captain…you don't strike me as a racist."

"I have a sister married to a Mexican who except for my father is the best man I've ever known. I worked with both a Kiowa and a Negro back in Texas. Fine, hard-working men, the both of them and I was proud to have them at my side when trouble came. The color of a man's skin means nothing to me."

"So what's your problem, then?"

"The enforcement of the law is not for dilettantes and amateurs. The Mayor thinks he's making Sovereign City safe allowing a bunch of would-be heroes with fancy names to run around taking the law into their own hands. They all think it's a lark to try and solve crimes and they're going to get innocent people killed one day if they keep interfering. And that includes McCall. Since you're McCall's mouthpiece I'll put you on notice then, I want to question him about Mr. An's murder. You tell McCall to come see me before I come to see him." Captain Lawman turned and stalked away back to the warehouse.

Eddie cocked an eye at his partner. "Can I get a professional opinion, Professor Lapinsky?"

Stephen shook his head slowly. "That there is a lad with issues, Mr. Padilla."

"Dangerous?"

"To himself more than anybody else. You think Fortune killed Mr. An?"

"Nah. An was okay. And you know Fortune…he doesn't kill unless he's forced to. Now if he looked at Tracy the wrong way, she'd shank him without a second thought but Fortune wouldn't let her do that."

"So what's our next move?"

"Go back to the car and report to Regina. Tell her to get an armed party ready and waiting. You and I will hang back and wait until the coppers clear out. Then we'll go inside the warehouse and conduct our own investigation."

—◦◦◦◦—

"Have you ever seen the like?" Tracy asked Fortune in wonderment.

"No. I have read of such but this is the first time I'm seeing it for myself."

After walking down the steeply slanting corridor for about five minutes, Fortune and Tracy came to a fork in the corridor. Upon taking the left fork, a stone slab descended from the ceiling, cutting them off from going back. They were forced to go on and soon emerged into a huge chamber, seemingly carved from the solid rock. Before them was a sight they had never expected to see.

The chamber was the entrance way to a dizzying series of hallways, corridors, and tunnels of various sizes. In the larger ones, shops and stalls did a thriving business. Vendors sold fruit that to Tracy's eyes looked fresh enough to have been picked that same day. Others sold vegetables or shish kebob lamb, chicken and fish cooked on charcoal braziers. Some of these were also living quarters. Shacks and huts of wood, tin, whatever could be thrown together for people to live in. Torches, huge flaming iron pots, and braziers were the only illumination.

Fortune pointed at the smoke from the huge pots. It spiraled upwards. "There's ventilation somewhere up there," he indicated the unseen ceiling.

"I'm more concerned that the locals don't seem surprised to see us. You would think they had visitors everyday based on their lack of attention."

Tracy was correct. Oriental men and women went about their business, pushing or pulling carts, shepherding children, hurrying along with their bundles. None gave as much as a curious look to Fortune and Tracy.

"About time you got here," a rough, husky voice behind them said. Fortune and Tracy turned to see a stooped over form a few feet behind them. Due to the rags wrapped around the face and head, it was impossible to tell if this was a man or a woman. The shapeless sack of a dirty blue cloak over the shoulders didn't help as well.

But Fortune knew well who it was. "Good of you to join us, Mrs. Lash."

Penelope stood up straight, unwrapping the rags from around her head. "Bother! How did you know it was me?"

"You've got your face all wrapped up so that no one can tell you are not Asian. Not hard to figure out."

"I could have been a leper."

"I don't think that in such close quarters, disease is tolerated. What do you think you are doing?"

"You and Miss Scott were taking your time slow poking around. I thought I'd best secure myself a disguise while waiting. Did you know all this was under here?"

"Not at all."

"I don't understand. Why would these people willingly live down here when they can live up top? In the fresh air and sunshine?"

"There are many reasons, Miss Lash but none we can go into right now." Fortune pointed at a group of determined looking men in black suits and fedoras shoving their way through the crowds of people right towards them.

Tracy grinned and cocked her .45. "Swell. All this sneaking around gets on my nerves. Give me a straight-up fight any day."

"You will put your weapon up. We're seriously outnumbered. We have no cover and no backup."

"You expect me to just hand over my guns without a fight?"

"I expect you to focus on why we're here. To find Mrs. Lash's husband. Speaking of which…" Fortune turned. As he expected, Penelope was no longer where she had been. The woman had an absolute genius for disappearing.

The Orientals surrounded Fortune and Tracy. She offered her .45's with poor grace while Fortune unstrapped his shotgun and handed it over. The leader grinned. "You show wisdom and respect. Continue to do so and perhaps your deaths will be painless."

Fortune and Tracy were escorted by their guard through the winding, narrow streets until they came to a blocky, four story building that looked as if it had been made for the sole purpose of withstanding a long siege. The windows were mere slits barely a foot wide. Just enough for machine gun barrels to be stuck out of.

The two of them were marched up the stairs and inside where they got another surprise. On the outside, the building looked about as decorative as a brick. But inside it was as richly decorated as a Mandarin's palace. Well lit with electrical lights that after the oppressive semi-darkness of the outside were like the difference between night and day. Rich tapestries hung on the walls and the pillars were works of art in their own right.

Sitting in an arm chair at the desk placed in the exact center of the room, a man spoke into a telephone. He glanced up at Fortune and Tracy as they were brought before him. He finished his conversation and hung up the phone. He was dressed in a black business suit like his men but he obviously was the leader.

"My name is Tsou. You are Fortune McCall. The young woman is your associate and bodyguard Tracy Scott."

"Interesting place you have down here."

"Indeed. You two are the first outsiders in fifty years to find your way down here. Most of our other visitors are brought against their will."

"We had no intention of disturbing you. We're merely trying to find Benjamin Lash."

Tsou nodded. "And you will see him presently. But first, a bit of business." Tsou waved a hand. "Have Wang brought before me."

Two of the black suited men dragged in a Wang who now looked nothing like the cold blooded murderer Fortune and Tracy had been chasing. No, this Wang had obviously been soundly beaten. Ugly bruises and welts stood out in harsh contrast to a skin that had gone gray from shock. The men stood him upright before Tsou.

"Mercy, master! Mercy, I beg of you!"

Tsou shook his head slowly. "You can expect no mercy from me, foolish one. Even when we were barefoot boys robbing drunken oafs in the back streets of Shanghai I told you then that your love of the knife would someday be your undoing. That day is today."

"But Mr. An spoke of the Ui Kwoon Ah-How to these unbelievers! He had to die!"

"Agreed. But it was not your decision to determine the manner of his death. Mr. An was a man of honor and respect, worthy of a clean death at the hands of an equal, not low-born scum such as you. By your killing him, you assured his soul of everlasting torment in The Hell of The Broken Brothers." Tsou motioned to the two men holding him. "Take him away. He has earned The Death of The Crimson Light."

Upon hearing that, Wang yowled as if he were already cast down into the deepest pit of Hell. He struggled as if taken by sudden insanity. Two more of the black suited men seized Wang's legs and lifted him clean up off the floor and carried him from the room. Wang screamed for mercy until it seemed as if his throat would burst. Even after he was carried past a thick wooden door that boomed shut, Fortune and Tracy could still hear his miserable screaming.

Fortune looked at Tsou. "I would take it that The Death of The Crimson Light is not at all pleasant."

"You take it correctly. Fortunately, you will not be subjected to it."

"Why not simply let us go? Along with Mr. Lash. You have my word we will not speak of this. All we want is to reunite the man with his wife. She's sick with grief."

"Alas, that is not an option. However, I must keep you until my master has given me a decision regarding you, Mr. McCall. You have very influential family ties and my master has several operations going on in that part of Africa you hail from. He would prefer not to incur the wrath of your father if it can be helped. However, you have also dared to interfere in the business of the Ui Kwoon Ah-How and that cannot be ignored."

Fortune grinned broadly. "My compliments to your intelligence network. I take it you know who I am, then?"

"I do."

"And you still will not take my word that I will say nothing of this?"

"And as I have already said, Mr. McCall, that decision has been taken from me. But I will see that your curiosity is satisfied." Tsou motioned again. "Place them in the same cell with Mr. Lash. And double the guard on the door."

Fortune bowed slightly. "I'm flattered you think me so formidable."

"The doubled guard isn't for you, Mr. McCall." Tsou pointed at Tracy. "It's for her."

The police had long gone. Captain Lawman apparently wasn't going to waste time, men, or resources on trying to track down Fortune McCall or in further investigation of the explosion in the fortune cookie factory. The body of Mr. An had been taken away to the City Morgue and the doors boarded up and affixed with the proper seals.

Eddie and Stephen had watched all this from their parked car. Perhaps an hour after the police departed, four black Packard sedans pulled up. Eddie and Stephen climbed out of their car and approached the four sedans.

Regina Mallory emerged from the lead car. Her rich waterfall of

THE MAGIC OF MADNESS

fiery red hair she had secured under a black military style beret. She herself was garbed all in black, hefting a Thompson submachine gun under one arm. A bandolier of spare clips draped across her shoulder.

From the rest of the cars emerged a dozen men, they too all wore black. They carried Thompsons like Regina as well as holstered .45 automatics. Foot long hunting knives with bone handles were also part of their arsenal as well as fighting spears called krussi that were similar to the feared Zulu Iklwa that had enabled the mighty Shaka Zulu to forge an empire. In addition they bore on their left arms tribal war shields. But instead of being made of animal hide, these elongated oval shields were of bulletproof steel. Despite their weight, the men carried them as easily as if they were made of paper. In addition, the shields had slits through which the barrels of the Thompsons could be extended, allowing the warrior behind the shield to fire at the enemy while being protected. These warriors were of the Otwani tribe that inhabited the North African country of Khusra. Warriors hardened in both battle and the region they chose to live in, a brutal and harsh desert known as The Devil's Anvil. It was there that the Otwani lived and had held their land for untold generations. The Otwani also were the personal guards and protectors of the Mwinyimkuu, the family that had ruled Khusra since the day when Nkosi lit the stars in the heavens with his fiery breath. Otwani men and women formed the primary compliment of the Heart of Fortune's crew.

The warriors spread out, forming a perimeter while their leader Mado spoke with Eddie. "Where be the Arao Onyagin?" he asked in a voice that sounded as if he had been chewing granite for breakfast, lunch and dinner since the age of two. At six foot six even, with football sized biceps and thighs like tree trunks Mado was every bit as formidable as he looked.

Eddie motioned for him to follow. "You brought explosives?"

"Of course."

"Because there's a stone door we have to blast through."

"Merely point us in the direction where the Arao Onyagin is being held by those foolish enough to do so and then stand aside while we express our displeasure."

ortune and Tracy were led to a cell that actually was a lot more comfortable and pleasant than either of them expected. Both of them had been in more than their share of similar situations and usually when they were told they were going to be thrown into a cell, that's exactly what they expected.

This cell however was nowhere near the dank, stone walled hole in the rock they anticipated. Instead, this was a well lit, goodly sized room with two beds, decent toilet facilities, a small bureau complete with mirror, a couple of reasonably comfortable chairs.

They also did not anticipate the wreck of a human being who lay on one of the beds. On stage, Benjamin Lash had been handsome and dashing. But now he looked nothing like that. His skin had lost its golden tan and now was lobster red. His eyes rolled wildly in their sockets. His broken pinky had been roughly set.

He screamed and scrambled off the bed, crawling on the floor on all fours like a huge, ungainly spider, slamming into a corner of the room. He clawed at the walls, howled like a dying animal.

Tracy kept far away from him, plainly disgusted. "What did they do to him, Fortune?"

Fortune did not answer. Instead he strode up to Lash and seized him by the shoulders and yanked him to his feet. Lash struck out with hands and feet, hissing and snapping. Fortune slapped him. Hard.

The blow was enough to shock Lash into being still. And that was all Fortune needed. He seized Lash by the head and forced Lash to look him directly in Fortune's eyes. "Benjamin Lash! I command you! Hugoiah hottotolaart ugostotla! Igosalek otorli!" Fortune's hands slid down to the back of Lash's neck manipulating key pressure points. "Listen to my words! Igosalek otorli!"

Lash slumped in Fortune's hands as if life had suddenly left his body. Fortune carefully eased him to the floor. Tracy timidly came closer. "You know you give me the creeps when you do stuff like that, right?"

"I had no choice. We need information and we need it fast." Fortune slapped Lash again. This time, lightly. "Come on, Benjamin! Wake up and speak!"

Lash lifted his head and looked up with wondering eyes at Fortune and Tracy. "Oh, my God. I wish I could tell you where I've been."

"Later for that," Tracy said. "We're here to help you but first you've got to help us. Why did these men take you? What do you have to do with them?"

THE MAGIC OF MADNESS

Lash gulped, fighting to talk around a dry tongue. "Diamonds. Five million dollars worth of diamonds I stole from the Ui Kwoon Ah-How. I've been smuggling diamonds around the world for them for years. I was the perfect courier as I was able to travel unmolested by the authorities. They never searched or inspected my luggage or equipment and even if they had, they'd never have found anything."

"How'd you get mixed up with a crowd like the Ui Kwoon Ah-How anyway?" Tracy demanded. "They don't seem like the outfit that would embrace white people into their loving bosom."

Lash smiled. "And that's where you're wrong. The Ui Kwoon Ah-How will make use of anybody willing to help them further their cause."

"And which cause is that, sir?" Fortune asked quietly.

"I don't know. I swear. All I know is that their master seeks massive wealth and influence. The Ui Kwoon Ah-How has power in places you wouldn't dream of."

"So what made you think you could steal from them?" Tracy demanded. "If they've got all this power and influence you claim they do, it's not exactly a smart move to rob them."

Lash laughed. It was an unpleasant laugh. The laugh of a man broken in spirit. "Greed, plain and simple. They paid me well, I won't deny that. But what they paid me was nothing compared to the value of the diamonds I smuggled. Finally, the temptation grew too great. Five million would enable me to purchase a new life for myself and Penelope, far away from the influence of the Ui Kwoon Ah-How. Australia or Africa, perhaps."

"You're a fool, Lash. Did you honestly think you would steal that much from them, from anybody and they would just let you get away with it?" Fortune demanded. "If this was just about you, fine. But you have involved your wife in this. She is sick with worry, thinking you are the injured, innocent party in this affair." Fortune shook his head. "You were already a wealthy man. You have a life and career that most can only dream of. And it still wasn't enough for you. You had to have more. And see where it has brought you."

Hearing a key in the lock of the door, Fortune and Tracy quickly took up positions on either side, intending to overpower whoever it was and take their weapons and make a try at escaping. The head that stuck itself into the cell was a welcome one, however.

Penelope Lash looked at Fortune with annoyance. "Aren't you supposed to be rescuing my husband? We're wasting a considerable amount of time with me having to rescue you." Then Penelope's eyes fell upon the ravaged face and body of her husband. With a cry of dismay she ran across the room to kneel at his side and embrace him. "Dear God, Ben! What have the bastards done to you?"

Tracy started forward. "Save your sympathy, sister. You need to know-" she stopped at the touch of Fortune's hand on her shoulder. He placed a gloved finger to his lips and motioned for her to step into the corridor.

The four men who had been guarding the cell were all unconscious. Their weapons lay near them. None of them had managed to get off so much as a shot or a cry of warning. Tracy bent down to retrieve her .45's which were stuck in the waistband of a guard's pants.

"Soon as we're finished with this caper, I'm going to have a good long talk with that woman."

"Jealous?"

"Jealous, hell. I'm gonna offer her a job. She took out these four men by herself, she's good. Not as good as me, but-" Tracy shrugged. "Who is? And why didn't you want me to tell her about her husband?"

"She wouldn't believe you and we don't have time right now to convince her. We've got to get out of here. Once back on the ship we can sort this all out."

"You have a plan?"

Fortune cupped a hand behind his ear. "Our rescue party should be here right...about...NOW."

Both of them heard a muffled explosion. Fortune grinned. "Unless I am wrong...that would be our friends with Mado and a squad of Otwani. Gather up the Lashes and let us go!"

After blasting their way through the thick stone door, the Otwani warriors arranged themselves into formation and trotted toward the underground settlement. They chanted the war songs of their tribe as there was no need for silence and stealth and in any case, the Otwani did not war without singing.

Gunshots spanged and ricocheted off the bulletproof steel shields as the Otwani ruthlessly returned the attack. The chattering of their Thompson submachine guns filled the underground air, joining with the screams of women pulling their children to safety and the curses of men diving for cover.

Regina, Eddie, and Stephen were safely in the middle of the Otwani formation. Much as they ached to be in the forefront of the battle, Mado had insisted. And one simply did not argue with Mado. It just wasn't done. Eddie yelled, "Mado! See that big building over there? You think they might have Fortune in there?"

"We will see," Mado replied and issued orders. As one, the squad of a dozen men swiveled around, double-timing it to the huge, blocky building. The black suited men had retreated to the safety of the building and closed up the doors. The smoking barrels of machine gun emerged from the narrow windows and unloaded a blizzard of lead upon the warriors.

The Otwani dropped into the classic Testudo formation, their shields overlapping to form an impenetrable defense.

"We can't stay here long!" Stephen shouted. "They'll regroup and attack us in force!"

Mado had already thought of that. He barked orders in their native language to the best spearman in the squad. The man worked with a fellow warrior quickly while the hail of deadly fire clanged against the bulletproof steel shields, sounding like a crew of madmen banging on a tin roof with hammers. At a barked order from Mado, a warrior stood up, his shield in front of him but still he took two bullets. But he had done his job, which was to provide cover for the warrior with the spear to hurl his weapon at the doors of the fortress. Secured to the shaft on the spear were two sticks of lit dynamite on short fuses.

The spear hit the door and two seconds later, the door disintegrated into splinters. With their war songs bursting from their lips, the Otwani charged. The black suited Orientals met them with equal ferocity. Broad bladed knives clanged against spearheads. Machine gun fire filled the huge inner chamber with smoke. Handguns barked. Oaths and curses in Mandarin and Cantonese mingled and mixed with Otwani chants in a weird song of death punctuating the wild fighting.

Eddie struggled hand-to-hand with an Oriental while yelling over his shoulder at Regina, "You and Mado go find Fortune and Tracy! Stephen and I will handle these guys!" Eddie delivered a devastating kick right where it hurt and his enemy yowled in overwhelming agony and dropped. Stephen stood side by side with the Otwani, firing his Thompson in short, controlled bursts that hit their targets, mowing down two or three of the enemy at the time.

Mado gestured to Regina. "If you are coming, then come!"
Regina nodded and ran after the huge warrior.

———✸———

Fortune and Tracy led the way up the corridor. The two of them supported Benjamin Lash between them as he was far too out of it to walk unassisted. Penelope Lash held one of Tracy's .45's in her hands and from the expert way she handled it, she'd had occasion to use handguns in the past.

"When we get outta this, I expect you to spill everything, sister," Tracy said.

"I don't know what you mean, Miss Scott."

"Come off it, lady. You took out four armed men without a sound. And those guys were better than good. You sneak around like a shinobi and I can tell you've handled guns before."

Penelope Lash grinned at the smaller woman, "Tell you what…you get my husband out of here and I'll come clean. Deal?"

"Deal!"

The group turned a corner and ran smack dab into Regina and Mado. Regina's Thompson came up in a flash before she saw who it was and she lowered the weapon with a grin of relief. "Fortune! Are you okay?"

"Yes, we're just fine, Regina," Tracy replied sarcastically. She handed over Benjamin to Mado. The big warrior slung Benjamin over one shoulder as if he weighed no more than a pound.

"You are well, Arao Onyagin? You were not harmed?" The terrible look in Mado's eyes promised wrath and woe undreamed of heaped on the heads of anyone who had done so.

"I am fine, faithful one. Discomfited somewhat and my ego bruised…which I shall address shortly. Come!"

The group raced back down the corridor to the huge inner chamber of the fortress. The black suited men of the Ui Kwoon Ah-How were still locked in deadly struggle with the Otwani. Despite the greater numbers of the Ui Kwoon Ah-How men, the discipline, superior weaponry, and sheer savagery of the Otwani had quickly turned the tide of battle in their favor. Across the room, Fortune spied Tsou clubbing one of his Otwani with a modified kanabo. A foot longer than a baseball bat, sheathed in iron with metal studs, the fearsome weapon easily smashed the clavicle of the warrior.

"Get clear," Fortune said to his friends in a voice that left no room for argument. He charged across the room, leaped up on top of Tsou's table, and launched himself up and over the heads of the combatants, right at Tsou. His duster billowed and flapped like a cape, his face obscured by the shadow of his fedora.

An experienced warrior, Tsou sensed the danger and whirled around, bringing up the kanabo to protect his head as Fortune came down. Fortune reached to the small of his back and removed something that had been hidden in a special pocket sewn into the interior lining of his tailored pants. As he came down, he raised that object, brought it down in a blur.

The kanabo splintered in half as if it were a twig, continuing on to break Tsou's left collarbone with an audible crack! that drowned out the sound of the kanabo. Fortune hit the ground, rolled, and came up on his feet. He spun around to face Tsou.

Held in Fortune's right hand was a mere, the fearsome Maori war club. Made of Nephrite jade, the leaf-shaped weapon was designed and perfect for close in-fighting.

Tsou dropped the two halves of his now useless weapon. "I don't suppose that we could negotiate a peaceful settlement?"

In response, Fortune's head gestured toward the downed Otwani warrior. Tsou nodded in understanding. With a wild yell, he threw himself at Fortune, right foot lashing out at Fortune's head.

Sidestepping with deceptive ease and grace, Fortune's mere whipped out to smash into Tsou's left side as he slipped under the kick. If Tsou hadn't already been disabled by Fortune's initial strike, that kick might have landed, so fast was he. Tsou landed heavily, groaning in pain from the cracked ribs. The mere was not a weapon to be taken lightly.

Fortune danced in, switching the mere rapidly from one hand to the other so as to confuse his enemy. As Tsou's eyes flickered back and forth between the moving weapon, Fortune suddenly dropped and swept Tsou's legs out from under him. Tsou hit the floor heavily, the entire left side of his body one huge hurt. He wouldn't have believed he could have been taken out so quickly. He lay there and watched as Fortune slowly got to his feet and stood over him.

"Mercy!" Tsou croaked.

"Did you show Benjamin Lash mercy? Or Wang? I fear that mercy is not something you have earned, my friend. And I do not subscribe to the practice of leaving an enemy alive. I detest having to look over my shoulder. And besides-" Fortune raised the mere over his head. "-I do not appreciate that you considered Tracy worthy of extra guards and not me."

The mere came down.

Fortune cleaned his weapon and joined his friends outside the fortress. Most of Tsou's men had broken off the fight and cleared out. The underground streets were empty of its denizens as they all were wisely hiding until the outcome of the fight. Fortune issued rapid orders to his men. "Collect our wounded and dead. Take all evidence that we were here."

Eddie gestured at the streets. "Fortune, what is this place? These people?"

"Time enough for explanations when we're back on the ship. Where is Mrs. Lash and her husband?"

"Over here, Fortune," Regina called. She stood a few feet away with Tracy at her side. And the both of them stood over a weeping Penelope Lash. She sat on the cold ground with her husband's head in her lap. She gently stroked his ravaged face. A face that even in death looked haggard and worn.

"When did he die?" Stephen asked quietly.

Tracy shrugged. "We were all so busy just trying to get out of there. Mado put him down here and went back into the fight. We were all busy covering each other…"

Fortune said, "Mrs. Lash?"

Penelope lifted her face, the tracks of her tears describing crooked trails through the soot and dust on her cheeks. "The big man…he put Ben down and told me to stay with him…Ben was choking, coughing… then he let out with one great big gasp and just…died."

Fortune looked at the woman for what seemed to be a long, long minute before turning about sharply, his duster billowing with the motion. "Come. Let us get back to the ship."

"But what about these people?" Regina said. "Surely we can't leave them here?"

Fortune's voice drifted over his shoulder, "Of course we can, Reggie. It's Chinatown."

Fortune McCall enjoyed many luxuries living on the top deck of The Heart of Fortune. Including a spacious, comfortable private lounge where he could entertain his guests and friends privately. It was being used now, some twenty-four hours later as a conference room to finally put to rest some remaining questions involving the Lash kidnapping.

Fortune was there, of course. Along with Eddie, Regina, Stephen, and Tracy. Penelope Lash sat in a comfortable armchair, dressed in black as befitting her widow's status. Chief Tate sat at a round polished mahogany table across from Fortune with Captain John Lawman at his side. And Captain Lawman did not look happy at all about anything.

"There's a dead man in the morgue, McCall," Captain Lawman said coldly. "A very famous dead man. The press and the public are demanding that justice be done."

The obviously worried Chief Tate put in, "A very famous dead white man who was murdered by Chinese criminals! I'm already getting pressure put on me to shut down Chinatown businesses until the man or men responsible for Mr. Lash's death are produced."

Fortune sat in utter relaxation, legs crossed, one arm hooked over the back of the chair he sat in. He smoked a thin, brown, hand-rolled cigarette that gave off exotic smelling blue smoke. He replied almost languidly, "Captain Lawman, you investigated the underground tunnels? You found the bodies of the Ui Kwoon Ah-How men?"

"I did."

"Then you have your murderers."

"Come on, McCall!" Chief Tate snapped impatiently. "You know full well how this works! We've got to have a live body! One we can parade around for the press to take pictures of and put on trial!"

"And take you off the hook," Eddie muttered.

"I heard that, Padilla! And you're damned right! I'm not that far away from my pension and I'm not risking getting that jammed up!"

Fortune gestured toward the silent Penelope. "I think you'd best listen to Mrs. Lash. I think that her statement will go a long way toward our deciding how this matter is best resolved."

Captain Lawman said, "Go ahead, ma'am."

Penelope lifted her veil. She was far more composed than she had been when she cradled her dead husband's head in her lap but her voice trembled noticeably when she said, "Gentlemen, what I am about to tell you may sound incredible but I assure you it is the truth. My husband

and I were working for The Department of Justice as undercover operatives."

"I don't believe a word of it!" Chief Tate cried out. "Preposterous! Why would a couple of stage magicians be asked to be spies by the government?"

"For exactly the same reason that the Ui Kwoon Ah-How would ask us to smuggle diamonds: we're internationally known celebrities. No one would ever suspect that such public entertainers would be secret agents or smugglers."

"It's along the same principal in a story by Edgar Allan Poe, gentlemen," Stephen Lapinsky said, his unlit pipe held loosely in his hands dangling between his knees. "It's about a stolen letter which the thief hides in plain sight. Even though the police can plainly see the letter, it never occurs to them that it's the one they're looking for because they assume the thief would hide such an important letter. The Lashes made the perfect undercover operatives. Nobody would ever dream of such well-known public figures of skullduggery."

Penelope nodded. "The Ui Kwoon Ah-How were indirectly responsible for the deaths of several Justice Department agents aboard. This was enough to bring them to the attention of The Justice Department who determined that steps should be taken to infiltrate this organization with an eye to wiping it out if they proved a credible threat to America.

"Benjamin and I were approached by a man we knew only as Intelligence One. He recruited us, personally supervised our training. He put out the rumor that due to gambling debts and poor investments, we needed money badly. The rumors were picked up by several criminal organizations and we did small smuggling jobs for them. These small jobs led us to the big fish, The Ui Kwoon Ah-How. We began working exclusively for them, transporting diamonds across Europe and into the United States. We also were able to put together a list of the Ui Kwoon Ah-How agents for Intelligence One."

"So you did the job you were recruited for, then." Captain Lawman frowned. There was something going on here but he couldn't see what it was. "I don't understand what the problem is."

"This last job the Lashes were doing for the Ui Kwoon Ah-How… it went wrong."

Chief Tate looked from Fortune to Mrs. Lash. "Wrong how?"

Penelope drew in a long, shuddering breath and just came out with it. "My husband really did steal those diamonds from The Ah Kwoon

Ah-How. He double-crossed them. He actually did intend on following through with his crazy plan."

"So that's why you didn't want to go to the police!" Regina said in sudden understanding. "That's why you wanted Fortune's help so badly!"

Penelope nodded. "I figured that if Mr. McCall could help me find the men who took Benjamin, I could do one of two things: persuade Ben that his plan was insane and return the diamonds or else, learn from him where he hid the stones and return them myself."

"Needless to say, things didn't work out the way Mrs. Lash planned-"

"-or you, for that matter," Eddie muttered again.

Fortune ignored him. "Gentlemen, I trust you see the problem. If this is revealed, The Justice Department will demand a full investigation into this and none of us want that." He blew out smoke. "My proposal is this: Mr. An is already dead. Regrettable, but a fact nonetheless. We place the blame for the Lash kidnapping on the unfortunate Mr. An. A straight-up kidnapping with the results being both the kidnapper and the kidnappee ending up dead."

Chief Tate and Captain Lawman swapped glances. Glances that obviously said more eloquently than any words that they were seriously considering this.

"Is there any way we can verify Mrs. Lash's story?" Captain Lawman demanded. He looked at Penelope. "Begging your pardon, Ma'am. I don't for a second mean to imply that you're lying about this. But-"

"I'm afraid you'll have to take my word for this, Captain. I've never known the true name of Intelligence One and he is the only one my husband and I had contact with. I have no way of knowing who else knew that Benjamin and I were working for him."

"My people have made inquiries, Captain," Fortune said. "They have ascertained that there is indeed a government operative using the codename Intelligence One. Beyond that, they could learn nothing else. The man's identity is known only to perhaps half a dozen White House staffers."

Captain Lawman looked skeptical. "And just how would your people have access to that kind of information?"

But Chief Tate waved that away as he asked, "Just one thing, McCall...how do we sell An's death? And Lash's?"

"Benjamin Lash, being an escape artist, got free of his bonds and heroically tried to escape from his captors. In the attempt, the two men struggled and killed each other."

And now Chief Tate nodded in satisfaction. "I like it. I can sell that."

"And what about The Chinatown Businessmen's Association?" Captain Lawman demanded. "They were friends with An. They're not going to like his name besmirched."

Fortune said quietly, "As if you truly care about what they think or what they'll do. You will tell them what is going to happen and they'll go along with it. They will not like it but the Chinese are a patient people. They will wait and bide their time for they know that the wheel turns and one day, it will turn in their favor."

Captain Lawman's eyes narrowed. "I don't much care for what you're implying, McCall."

"And I remind you, sir that you are on my ship. The thing you should be caring about at this moment is not disrespecting me."

"Come on, Captain. Our business here is done," Chief Tate said impatiently. "Thanks, McCall. We'll sell it exactly as you laid it out."

Captain Lawman stood, his fiery eyes locked into Fortune's calm ones. They held the gaze for a full minute, and then Captain Lawman followed Chief Tate out of the lounge.

"Y'know," Tracy said slowly. "I might be wrong but if I'm any judge it's my thinking that one day you're going to have to kill that man or he's going to kill you first."

"Perhaps. But that is another concern for another day." Fortune abruptly stood up and walked over to where Penelope sat. "Mrs. Lash? Is there anything else that I or my associates can do for you?"

"No. You've done far, far more than I ever could have expected."

"What are your immediate plans?"

"I'm going to bury Benjamin here. He doesn't have much family…a brother who he hasn't seen or spoken to in ten or eleven years…a few cousins…an aunt and uncle down in Florida. He wasn't close to any of them. I'll wire them out of courtesy."

"And you? You will continue to perform? Work with the government?"

"I…" Penelope blinked rapidly, dropped her eyes in momentary confusion. "I really can't say right now. So much has happened so quickly. I need a few days to really process what's happened, sort out my feelings, and decide where I want to go from here."

THE MAGIC OF MADNESS

"I quite understand. Please don't hesitate to call on me if I can be of further service. Eddie, would you please escort Mrs. Lash to the shore? Take a car and drive her wherever she wants to go."

"Sure, Fortune." Eddie gallantly offered his arm for Penelope to take. The two of them left the lounge and when they were walking down the stairs to the main deck, Fortune turned to the others.

"Stephen, Reggie…the two of you get some sleep. I'll need you to be in charge of the ship this evening. I will be out and I do not know how long I will be." Fortune looked at Tracy. "You'll be with me."

Tracy jerked her head at the chair Penelope Lash had been sitting in. "This got anything to do with the grieving widow? I saw how you were looking at her."

Fortune nodded slowly. "It does indeed have to do with Mrs. Lash. But not in the way you think…"

⥇⥇⥇

Enshrouded in darkness, The Croxton Opera House had no performances that night. Out of respect to Benjamin Lash, who had performed his last illusion there, the owners had announced in a press conference earlier that day that The Croxton would be closed for three days.

But inside, there was activity.

A slim form, masked and dressed all in black moved through the dim backstage storage areas with as much ease as if the backstage had been fully lit. Occasionally, this figure utilized a small flashlight no bigger than a fountain pen to illuminate and identify the objects stored away. Scenery, backdrops, fake trees, stuffed animals. Huge chests, racks and racks of costumes. And the equipment used by Benjamin and Penelope Lash in their magic act. The equipment had been placed here at Penelope's request until she made a decision as to what to do with it. Rumor had it she was going to sell the paraphernalia to a Rumanian magician and retire.

The slim figure bent over a clothing chest, opened it. Long fingers reached out to undo a secret catch. The light shone on a small leather bag hidden inside a secret box. The fingers opened the bag and upended it so that several objects tumbled into the other waiting hand.

They lay in the palm of that hand, sparkling like miniature stars.

Brilliant blue-white diamonds the size of grapes.

The overhead lights came on, filling the storage area with blazing white light. The slim form came upright with a gasp.

Fortune McCall stood no more than a few feet away, garbed in his fedora and duster. The upper half of his face, obscured by the shadow of his hat's brim, couldn't be read. But his easy smile of triumph could plainly be seen.

The slim figure turned to flee. And turned right into the muzzles of twin .45 automatics held in the small, but more than capable hands of Tracy Scott. "You can take off the mask, sister. It's over."

A gloved hand went up to snatch off the mask, revealing the beautiful face of Penelope Lash. She looked at Fortune. "How did you know?"

"Your husband dying. I didn't have time to examine him fully but his heartbeat was strong. Yes, he had been tortured and put through a considerable amount of pain. But Tsou needed him alive and in shape to tell where he hid the diamonds. He should not have died. Unless, of course, you killed him." Fortune gestured at the diamonds Penelope poured back into the small bag. "What's the real story, Penelope? You and Benjamin were in it together? The both of you stole the stones from the Ui Kwoon Ah-How? And when he was kidnapped you needed help to find him so you duped me into helping you. Is that how it was?"

"Mr. McCall…Fortune…it wasn't like that at all. I swear to you that Benjamin stole the diamonds on his own."

"You didn't appear to have much of a problem finding them."

"We have plenty of secret compartments in our trunks and chests. I just happened to be lucky and they were in the first one I picked."

"I don't buy it, Fortune," Tracy said quietly.

"Listen to me! After I left your ship and returned to my hotel I contacted Intelligence One and informed him of what happened. He instructed me to find the stones and use them to finance an operation here in Sovereign City to investigate the Ui Kwoon Ah-How further. He's going to send two more of his operatives to assist me in this."

"I'm telling you, Fortune, don't trust her!" Tracy insisted. "She's resourceful and clever. Remember how quickly she was able to improvise a disguise in that underground hideout? And she took out four armed men by herself? How she's able to get around unseen? I'm telling you, there's more to her than she's letting on."

"If you had a method of contacting Intelligence One, why didn't you inform Chief Tate and let him talk to the man, verify your bona fides?"

"That's not how Intelligence One operates, Fortune."

"You appear to have an extreme amount of loyalty toward this man."

Penelope smiled widely. "At times it feels like he's a father to me."

Fortune smiled back. "I think I understand. So, what are we to do with you?"

"Let me go. The story you cooked up to explain Benjamin's death is a good one and Intelligence One will back it up all the way. In the meantime, I'll be ferreting out the Ui Kwoon Ah-How here in Sovereign City with the help of the other two agents. And I'll make them pay for what they've done to me and Benjamin."

Tracy groaned in exaggerated disgust. "I say we either shoot her or turn her over to Tate. Last thing this cockamamie city needs is another self-appointed do-gooder."

Penelope Lash suddenly did the last thing either Fortune or Tracy expected. She dropped down so low that her buttocks brushed the rough wood floor and then she sprang straight up into the air. The two of them were taken completely by surprise. Penelope's laughter drifted downward and they heard her rapidly receding footsteps clattering on the metal catwalk that had to be at least ten feet above their heads.

"Well, I'll be damned," Tracy gulped, stowing away her automatics. "You think you could do that?"

Fortune shook his head. "Not on my best day. You?"

"Hell, no. It takes years of physical and mental conditioning to be able to do something like that. I'm the best that the Irulani Temple has trained in ninety years and I couldn't pull that off."

"Who could?"

Tracy shrugged. "Take your pick. If I had a chance to take her on hand-to-hand I could identify which style she uses, where she was trained."

"You may yet have your chance. Something tells me we have not seen the last of our Mrs. Lash." Fortune motioned to Tracy. "Come, cousin. We've got a casino to run."

Tracy fell into step next to Fortune. "You still got the whim-whams for her?"

"No. I think that if and when we run into her again that I shall most definitely be keeping my distance from Penelope Lash. Based upon what happened to the late Mr. Lash, I think that she does not take kindly to relationships that do not live up to her high expectations."

THE
GOLD
OF
BOX
850

◆

THE GOLD OF BOX 850

Due to the level of noise in the casino, Fortune McCall didn't hear every word Tais Pennington-Smythe said but he most certainly did hear the last one. He removed the Macanudo cigar from his mouth and said quizzically, "Did you say gold?"

Tais smiled, cocked her head playfully to one side. "I did."

"How much gold are we talking about?"

"A lot."

"Fortune shrugged. "I've seen a lot of gold in my time, Tais. You will have to be more precise than that."

"Between three and five million dollars worth."

And now Fortune really was interested. "I think we'd best retire to somewhere a bit more private so that we can discuss this comfortably." Fortune gestured for Tais to follow him. They walked past rows of gleaming slot machines and made a left at the card tables. Saturday nights were usually the best for The Heart of Fortune and this Saturday night was no different. The poker, roulette, and faro tables were packed. Every slot machine's arm was being worked with a will and in the adjacent dining room, diners and dancers were being entertained by Monarch Redfern and His Orchestra playing "By A Waterfall."

Fortune caught the eye of Pasquale Zollo, standing near the cashier's cage. It was Pasquale's turn to be pit boss, a job that rotated between Pasquale, Eddie Padilla, Stephen Lapinsky, and Regina Mallory.

Through gestures, Fortune indicated that he would be in his office if needed.

Fortune's office would have wrung envy from a bank president. He walked over to a huge globe standing in a corner, opened it up to reveal a fully stocked bar contained within. "Champagne? Brandy?"

"I'm in a brandy mood tonight, thank you." Tais took off her gloves, placed them on top of her purse and dropped them all casually on Fortune's desk before seating herself in the leather armchair in front of the desk.

"Good. I have some very excellent Braastad I've been looking for an excuse to drink. Half a moment, please." Fortune poured them drinks, handed Tais her snifter and he then settled into the comfortable high-backed leather chair behind his mahogany executive desk. "Elaborate on this gold. And please don't leave out any details." Fortune grinned as he placed his cigar in a marble ashtray.

"You know I'm still working for Box 850 with the full cooperation of the United States government and Sovereign City authorities?"

"I was informed of such by Mayor Byles. After that caper with the Mayhews, you went to Washington for debriefing and it was agreed by Washington and London that you should return here and root out the Mayhews."

Tais sipped her brandy, nodded. "Exactly. To that end, Box 850 contacted one Herbert Hornsby, president of the Hornsby Loan and Trust. Hornsby served in The Great War and afterwards, took over the family business. He is notable for opening international branches in New York, Paris, Macao, and here in Sovereign City. It was felt that Hornsby could be brought into confidence."

"To what end?"

"Box 850 has been operating here in the States for a considerable amount of time. Some of those operations have been conducted jointly with the Americans. Even more haven't. Those operations needed to be funded. Box 850 has a network of British bankers operating branches of their institutions here in the States. These bankers were trusted with the funds necessary to keep those operations running."

"I suppose even spies have to pay rent. What does this have to do with gold?"

"I'm getting to that. May I have another drink, please? All this infernal talking dries the tongue so, don't you know."

Fortune hauled himself up out of his seat as if it were the most laborious task in the world. He took the snifter from Tais, saying, "The gold?"

"I'm coming to that. Due to the threat of the Mayhews as well as others across the country, it was determined that Box 850's activities needed to be increased. This would involve a restructuring of the funding method. Hornsby was selected as the man to oversee and supervise the restructuring."

Fortune handed her a fresh drink. "Let me guess. Our Mr. Hornsby proved to not be as trustworthy as he was thought to be."

"Correct. Apparently what he did was restructure a considerable amount of those funds into gold. Gold he had brought here to Sovereign City for some unspecified reason."

"How do you know all this?"

"We got that much from Hornsby's assistant. He broke down under interrogation and gave us the information I've just told you."

"Where is the assistant now?"

"Under secure guard, I assure you."

"So where's the gold?"

"The assistant doesn't know. Hornsby told him just enough to get his help to cover the theft. He doesn't know much more outside of what I've just told you."

"So why not just interrogate Hornsby?"

"Because Herbert Hornsby was found dead in his office just a few hours ago. Murdered. Somebody beat him to death. Presumably because they wished to know where the gold was."

"You think Hornsby gave up the information?"

"I don't know. But until I do, I'm under orders from Box 850 to proceed as if he didn't and recover that gold."

"So why come to me? You've got the resources of Sovereign City's police at your disposal. And didn't I read something in the society column of the papers that you've been seen out to dinner with Lazarus Gray? Why not ask him for help? Or Machine McQueen?"

"Don't believe everything you read in the papers. And you know full well why I've come to you for help. I know you. I know your skills and your capabilities. We've worked together before. If there's anybody I trust to help me recover five million dollars worth of gold, it's you."

"I know all that. I just like to hear you say it." Fortune tilted back his head, blew cigar smoke up at the ceiling. He appeared to be deep in thought. He finished the rest of his drink and looked back at Tais. "Ten percent."

Tais blinked. "Beg pardon?"

"My finder's fee. Ten percent of whatever we recover."

"Why you cheap, grifting, two-cent hustler-"

"That ten percent will go a long way to helping Sovereign City's poor and underprivileged. I will of course provide you with a list of the charities I donate the ten percent to so that you will know the money was spent well."

"Oh." Tais blinked again. A third time. When she spoke, her voice was a bit more contrite. "No, that won't be necessary. Your word has always been good enough for me. But here's the problem. Officially, I can't make such a bargain. That gold belongs to Box 850 and they trust me to recover it."

"And unofficially?"

"Let's just say that if and when we find the gold, I'd be willing to leave you to keep an eye on it while I went to the ladies room for five minutes."

"Good enough." Fortune stood up. "Well! Allow me to have another drink, inform Pasquale that I will be going ashore and then we can get this treasure hunt started!"

———— ∞ ————

Herbert Hornsby's residence in The Delroy Arms was quite modest and downright frugal. Fortune stood in the foyer as Tais went through the apartment, turning on lights. Fortune took off his storm cloud gray fedora and tossed it carelessly to hang on the hat rack. He left his duster and gloves on.

"Have you searched this apartment?" Fortune asked, merely looking around, taking in everything.

Tais emerged from the bedroom. "Not as yet. I did search his office. I found nothing. But I did have guards posted outside to make sure nobody entered until I had a chance to talk to you."

"Yes, the two gentlemen outside in the hall look quite formidable. I doubt that they would let anybody get by them." Fortune walked over to join her in the bedroom. They both knew that the places to start a search of anybody's house or apartment were the bedroom and bathroom. Efficiently, quietly, they went to work.

It was while Fortune was in the process of looking for a wall safe that he stopped and said, "Hasn't it struck you as odd that we haven't found any personal papers at all? Much less business papers."

"And there's no family pictures, either," Tais replied. Her voice muffled as she was looking under the bed. She came upright, leaned on the bed. "In fact, there's nothing of a personal nature at all in this apartment."

"Exactly. Are you thinking what I'm thinking?"

"This isn't where Hornsby actually lived."

Fortune rubbed his chin absently, nodding in agreement. "Which means that we are wasting valuable time here while Hornsby's killers are getting closer to the gold. Assuming that they got the information from him."

"Let's not assume anything, okay? Especially not that."

"Let me ask you something. Did Hornsby have a wife?"

"Good question. Let me make some calls." Tais went into the living room, used the telephone there. After three phone calls she had her information, turned back to Fortune. "Hornsby is indeed married but his wife is back in England. She left Sovereign City three years ago."

"Interesting. What's her maiden name?"

Tais frowned. "I didn't ask all that. Why?"

"Just find out, will you, please?"

With a frown of annoyance, Tais used the phone again and found out in less than two minutes. "Green. Now what's this all about?"

Fortune now himself used the telephone to call The Heart of Fortune where he asked for Eddie Padilla to be put on the phone.

"Fortune, where the hell are you? The gang and I don't appreciate you going off on a caper, taking only Ronald and cutting the rest of us out of the action."

"I don't even know if there is any action to be had but if there is, trust me, you will be the first to know. But right now I need you to find out if there are any apartments or houses in Sovereign City in the names of Hornsby or Green. And I need that information fast, Eddie. I'll be in the Cadillac so contact me by radiophone."

"Gotcha. Soon as I get something, you'll know. Just don't forget the rest of us!"

Fortune chuckled as he hung up the phone. Tais was still frowning. Somehow on her frowns didn't look as severe as they did on most other women. "And what's all that about?"

"It's not out of the realm of possibility that your trusted banker rented or bought another residence and that is where a clue may be found."

"Sovereign City is huge. Or haven't you noticed? It could take Eddie days to get that information!"

"If he doesn't have it in an hour, I'll be very surprised. We've only been here a relatively short time but Eddie has built up a surprisingly efficient network of informants in the Latin and Negro communities. There are hundreds of thousands of eyes that see, ears that hear. And nobody pays any attention to them. Porters, elevator operators, maids, custodians, janitors, dishwashers, cooks, domestic servants...they all see and hear things that are of extraordinary value they will share. If you have their trust and they know that the giving of that information will not fall back on them."

"They know Eddie works for you?"

"But of course."

They were walking out of the apartment, toward the elevators. Tais paused to issue instructions to the two guards and then rejoined Fortune and continued their conversation.

"Seems to me that they wouldn't be so quick to help you. I mean, you're rich and they're not."

"You still have a lot to learn about people, Tais. And we have legitimate sources of information as well. We'll have the information soon, never fear."

In front of The Delroy Arms, a long black Cadillac waited, the finely tuned engine barely purring. Ronald Scocco sat behind the wheel, a cap pulled low over his forehead. As Fortune and Tais climbed into the rear of the machine he asked, "Everything okay, boss?"

"We found nothing here, Ronald. We're waiting on information from Eddie and might as well grab something to eat while we wait. Take us over to Honeychile's on Nash Avenue."

Unseen by Fortune, Ronald, or Tais, a pair of angry eyes observed them from the safely of a darkened doorway across the street. The eyes followed the Cadillac as it smoothly pulled away from the curb. A slender man stepped out of the doorway, his face obscured by the upturned collar of his trench coat and pulled down hat. He walked rapidly two blocks until coming to a drugstore. He entered and went straight to the row of telephone booths in the rear. He went in one, closed the door and made his call.

"It's me, Bobby. Yeah. The dame came back to the limey's place.

No. She wasn't alone. Get this, she was with a colored guy. No, I ain't been drinkin'. A colored guy, dressed as fancy as a white man in a tux and a long coat that he didn't buy offa the rack. Shut up and listen a minnit, willya? I think he was Fortune McCall. Yeah, the colored guy what owns the gambling ship. Yeah, well, he's been getting' a rep in Sovereign as somebody it ain't smart to monkey with. Colored or not, he's bad medicine. Yeah, yeah, I know what the payoff in this deal is. I'm just tellin' you-" The thug fell silent as the voice on the other end apparently was saying something Bobby wanted to hear. Gradually, a smile appeared on the thug's face, getting wider and wider.

"Well, hell! Why didn't you say so in the first place? If I'd known that's what you got fixed up I wouldn't have worried in the first place. Okay, I'll head back to the hideout. Yeah. Yeah. Okay, see you soon."

"I would never have guessed this could taste so good." Tais said for perhaps the tenth time. "If you had told me before tonight that chicken and waffles tasted so good together, I'd have told you that you were crazy."

Fortune grinned at her, pleased she enjoyed her food so thoroughly. No need to ask if Ronald Scocco was enjoying his meal. The boy had torn through two complete helpings and was working on his third as if he hadn't eaten for a week.

Tais eyed Ronald with a look akin to amazement. The boy appeared to be no thicker than a broom handle with pipe-stem arms and legs. But he was packing away enough food for three men three times his size as if he did it everyday.

"Frightening, isn't it?" Fortune said. He knew exactly what Tais was thinking. "I have had Ronald checked out by a number of doctors. They say he's fine. Just a normal growing boy."

"He keeps eating like that he's going to grow outrageously and that's a fact."

Ronald looked up from his plate and winked. "Hey, I like to eat. There's worse habits I could have."

"Indeed," Fortune signaled to their waiter for more coffee.

Honeychile's was known throughout Sovereign City for its genuine southern cooking. The owner, a wide-hipped woman who everybody knew only as Sowhat presided over the kitchen and restaurant like a Russian duchess with her loud, brassy voice that could and had stopped two hundred pound coppers in their tracks. Rumor had it she had been a mistress of the great Harlem gangster Bumpy Johnson and had even run her own lucrative numbers racket in Brooklyn before accidentally killing her own sister in an argument over a man. That's when she came to Sovereign.

Not knowing what the rest of the night held in store for them, Fortune had suggested they all get a good solid meal inside of them while they waited for Eddie to get back to them.

"Where did you meet Ronald anyway?" Tais asked.

Fortune looked at the boy. "Do you mind?"

"Nah. I'm long past it. And Miss Pennington-Smythe is okay."

Fortune took a sip of coffee before talking. "I was in Chicago on business about three years ago. One night I'm driving along a street near Riverview Park when I saw Ronald being attacked by three boys obviously older and bigger than he was at that time. I stopped my car and got out to help. Turns out that Ronald didn't need my help. He soundly and efficiently beat the hell out of all three boys and sent them running home to their mothers. I asked him if he were hungry, he said yes and so I took him to dinner. He's been with me ever since."

"Didn't his parents have something to say about that?"

"My pa run away from home," Ronald said. He wiped his mouth with his napkin and took a deep swallow of his tall glass of milk before continuing. "My ma wasn't no good after that. Kept saying that he must have got into an accident and was lying in a hospital somewhere. Or he was dead in a ditch. She always liked to pull a cork but after Pa run off she really hit the hootch. After a week or two she told me to stay in the 'partment until she came back. Said she was going to find Pa." Ronald shrugged. "She never came back. The food run out but the neighbors fed me until the landlord changed the locks and told me to go to the orphanage. I lived on the streets for a couple of days, hangin' around the neighborhood in case Ma or Pa came back. When the boss found me I had wandered on down to Riverview just to have something different to do."

"That's horrible! Fortune, why didn't you try and find his parents?"

"I did. I still am. I have the best private investigative agency in Chicago on permanent retainer. They have been looking for Ronald's parents all this time. They have instructions to find them be they alive or be they dead."

"When they're found they should both be horsewhipped."

"Aw, that's okay," Ronald gulped down more milk, wiped away the mustache with the back of his other hand. "I'm not mad any more at them. I guess they did what they thought they had to do. And I'm with Fortune, now. He takes real good care of me. Got me a tutor and everything to educate me. Gave me a home and friends. And Pasquale's family treats me like I was one of them so I guess I got a family in the deal as well. I didn't make out so bad."

Fortune smiled and said, "Ronald, go check the radiophone in the car. See if Eddie's got something for us."

"Sure thing, Fortune." Ronald pushed back his chair and made his way through the crowded restaurant toward the door. Tais watched him go.

"That's a good thing you did for that boy, Fortune. What are you going to do when his parents are found?"

"They were found."

"But you just said-"

"Tais, Ronald's father is dead. Killed by a jealous husband. His mother is in Kansas City, working in a whorehouse. Now, you tell me. Should I tell him that?"

"Fortune, he deserves to know the truth."

"Yes he does. And one day I will tell him."

"Do the others know?"

"No. Only I know the truth. And now, so do you."

Tais gave him a serious, penetrating look. "You know, I like you, Fortune. A lot. You're a good man with a generous heart that's in the right place. But I have to be honest with you: you're a man who enjoys his secrets far too much. Everybody's got secrets. That's a fact of life. But you relish the ones you have. And those of others."

"Tais, contrary to popular opinion, the truth does not always set you free. Sometime it's a prison more confining and restrictive than any built by man." Fortune abruptly stood up. "But this is a philosophical discussion we have to pick up at a later date. Ronald's waving for our attention."

"You go ahead, I'll take care of the bill."

"No need. I have an arrangement with Sowhat. Let's go see what Ronald has for us." Fortune did leave a generous tip for their waiter, who bowed in thanks.

Outside, Ronald already had the Cadillac running. He sat behind the wheel, leaned over to speak to Fortune through the open passenger window. "Eddie's got an address for the Hornsby guy. The house is in his wife's maiden name just like you figured."

"You know where it is?"

"I can have you there in thirty minutes."

"Make it fifteen."

⸻ ◌◦◌ ⸻

Ronald stopped in front of a one-story bungalow with earth tone shingles. No lights burned. The rest of the block was quiet. Fortune leaned forward to talk to Ronald. "Best not sit here with the motor running. We don't want to tip off anybody that might show up. Find someplace close enough for you to watch the house. If anything happens, use your own judgment as to how to proceed."

Ronald nodded. Fortune and Tais walked up to the front door. She gave the knob a turn. "Locked."

"Well, of course it is. Let me at it." Fortune already had his lock pick set in his hands and in forty seconds flat, they were standing inside. Tais flicked on the lights.

"Now this is more like it," Tais said with satisfaction.

It was quite apparent that somebody did indeed live here. A Zimmerman baby grand piano stood over in front of the picture window, the top covered with elegantly framed photographs. More photos hung on the walls along with various documents. Coats hung on the coat rack. In the kitchen, a pair of dishes and glasses sat in the sink. In the bathroom and bedroom there was even more evidence of the place having been lived in. The bed was even unmade.

Tais opened the door of the bedroom closet and began rummaging around inside. "I've got women's clothes in here as well as men's."

Fortune, from the other side of the bedroom where he opened bureau drawers and went through them rapidly replied, "Women's undergarments here as well. Are you sure that the wife didn't return to Sovereign?"

"Positive. Which means that Hornsby had himself a little chippie on the side. Let's take a look at those photos on the piano."

The two of them did so. Some of them were of Hornsby by himself or with what most likely were various family members. Several pictures depicted him with a matronly women and three mournful looking children, a boy and two girls. "Hornsby's wife and children?" Fortune ventured.

"Undoubtedly. Look at those faces. The kids look as miserable as their pop. But he doesn't look miserable with her." Tais passed over a picture in an ornate silver frame, obviously expensive. It was a big difference from the plain wooden frames the pictures of Hornsby's wife and children were in.

The woman standing next to Hornsby in the picture was a knockout, to put it plainly. And next to her, Hornsby had a grin on his face so wide it threatened to split his head in two.

"Pig," was Tais' opinion.

"If I had a woman who looked like that on my arm, I'd be grinning like an idiot as well."

"That's because you're a man and men are pigs. Let's search the rest of this place. Maybe we can find out the name of this home wrecking hussy."

———∞———

Ronald had parked in the driveway of a house three doors down and across the street. A careful reconnoitering of the house assured him that whoever lived there was not home. No empty milk bottles had been placed out on the front porch for the milkman to replace in the morning which was a further welcome sign that the occupants had stopped their milk delivery. So Ronald parked there, cut the lights and engines and kept an eye out.

However, that didn't mean he didn't have problems of his own. Tracy called him on the radiophone and proceeded to give the boy eight different kinds of hell.

"Ronald, I am giving you a direct order. You tell me exactly where you and Fortune are."

"Sorry, Trace…can't do it. Fortune gave me orders not to tell you guys where we are or what we're doing."

"You're going to be in so much trouble when you get back on this boat, buster!"

"Trace, you know I love you like a sister. But whaddya want me to do? Fortune's the boss."

"Ronald, all we want to do is help! What's so wrong with that?

Whatever you and Fortune are doing, wouldn't it be better if you guys had some backup?"

"To be honest, Trace, I think he's enjoying being on a caper with Miss Pennington-Smythe."

"Well, of course he is! That's the problem! You've seen what happens when he gets twisted up with her! Now I'm not going to argue with you any more, young man! I'm older than you and I demand-"

"Sorry, Trace! Gotta go! I think something's about to happen!"

"Ronald J. Scocco! Don't you dare-"

Too late. Ronald broke the connection and hung up the handset. A car had turned the corner, slowly coming down the street toward the Hornsby house. What had caught Ronald's attention were the car's headlights going out as it approached the Hornsby house. Ronald slid down a bit further in the seat, never taking his eyes off the car. The driver stopped the car. The doors opened and four men got out. Quickly, silently, two of them made their way to the back while the other two headed for the front door. Ronald waited until they barged in the door. He then opened up his door and crept out. Keeping low, he ran across the street.

—⊗≋⊗—

"**Y**ou just keep yer hands where we can see 'em." The two men stood there with guns in their hands pointed at Fortune and Tais. They'd been caught flatfooted, paying too much attention to their search of the house and not enough to watching their backs.

One of the men, an unlovely specimen with suspicious, narrow eyes said nastily, "Where's the gold? We know you musta found out where it is."

"And you are…?" Fortune asked.

The man with the suspicious eyes spat on the floor in front of Fortune. "I ain't talkin' to you, nigger. And you might as well start strippin' while the bitch talks. Them's white man's clothes you got on. Take 'em off."

While his slightly smiling face never changed expression, Fortune's left eyebrow raised. From behind him, he heard two more men who had come in the back way. "Nobody else here, Paulie."

"Good deal." Paulie raised his .38 and pointed it at Tais. "Now. I ain't gonna ask again. Where's that gold?"

"Answer his question first," Tais snapped back. "Who are you? Who are you working for?"

"Shit. I got no time for this," Paulie snarled. "Beetle! Take out yer knife and cut one'a the nigger's ears off. Maybe that'll make her talk."

The picture window shattered as a fist sized rock came hurtling through it. It sped across the room with unerring accuracy to hit Paulie right in the forehead, stunning him enough to make him drop to his knees, his gun clattering away.

Fortune whirled around, his hand going to the lower of the only two buttons on his duster. One at his left shoulder, the other at his left hip. With fluid, practiced ease, he undid the button. At the same time, the twisting of his body unsnapped the sawed-off Browning A-5 pump shotgun from the clip on his belt. Swinging from a lanyard, the shotgun slapped into his waiting gloved hands. The shotgun whoomed twice, both shells taking Beetle and his partner square in their chests, knocking them right out of the living room into the kitchen.

Tais reached into her purse and withdrew a silver plated .45 automatic and placed a bullet in the knee of Paulie's partner who stood there, slack jawed with amazement at how fast things had turned around. He collapsed to the floor, howling.

Ronald burst in through the back door. Hardly sparing a glance at the two dead men on the floor, he vaulted over them, into the living room, a cocked and ready .38 in his hand. "You okay, boss?"

Fortune grinned at the boy. "Yes. Thanks to you. Quick thinking with that rock."

"I figured a distraction was the best play instead of just busting in, guns blazing."

"Remind me to give you a raise." Fortune walked over to Paulie. He crawled on the floor, wiping away at the blood pouring into his eyes from the sizeable gash in his forehead caused by Ronald's thrown rock with one hand while the other sought his gun.

Fortune delivered a forceful kick to Paulie's midsection that lifted him up off the floor. He twisted in mid-air, came crashing back down with enough force to expel air from his lungs. Fortune placed a foot on Paulie's chest. "Would you care to resume our exchange of information now, sir?"

Paulie spent the next minute giving explicitly concise and profane directions as to where Fortune could go and what he could do to himself once he arrived.

"I see that we'll have to take this to the next level, then." Fortune swung his shotgun back in place and secured the clip. "Ronald, escort Tais to the car and bring it round to the front of the house, if you please. Mr. Paulie and I need to have a private chat."

When Ronald didn't answer right away, Fortune looked around to see what he was doing. Ronald held the silver framed picture in his hand. "Hey, I know her."

"You do?" Tais asked in amazement. "How do you know her? Where?"

"She's Wilma Cole. She sings at The Choco Club."

Fortune and Tais swapped looks. It was Fortune who continued. "Ronald, how do you know that?"

"Eddie and Pasquale had me drive them over to that club a couple of times last month. You remember that Pasquale recommended you hire a singer for a couple of nights a week. They went around to a buncha clubs scouting out singers. She's one'a them."

"Well, I'll be damned," Tais said. "Let's get over there!"

"You go ahead with Ronald. I still need to chat with my friend here."

Tais looked hard at Fortune. "Look here, Fortune...those two men...that was self-defense. You kill this man and that's murder, plain and simple. And I won't have it."

"I have no intention of killing this man. I want to talk to him and find out who he works for and how they know about the gold."

"Then why can't we stay here while you question him?"

Ronald lightly took Tais by the elbow. "Miss, it's better if we do as the boss says. Trust me on this."

Reluctantly, Tais allowed Ronald to lead her outside.

Fortune slowly took off his gloves as his eyes locked on Paulie's. "And now, sir...let's you and I talk..."

As they walked to the car, Tais said, "Ronald, give it to me straight: what is Fortune going to do to that man?"

"Talk to him, Ma'am." Ronald plainly didn't want to elaborate any further.

"Ronald, I want a straight answer!"

"And I gave you one, Ma'am." Ronald stopped and turned around, looking her directly in the eyes. "And it's the only one you're gonna get from me cause Fortune looks after me. Not you. Now, I like and respect you a lot 'cause you're his friend. But don't ask me to tell on him. You wanna know anything more than what I told you, you ask him."

The two of them remained silent as they climbed into the Cadillac. Ronald started it up and drove slowly to the front of the house. Tais listened carefully for the sound of a shotgun blast and heard none. And as Fortune walked out of the house, tugging on his gloves she saw no evidence of blood on his clothes that surely would have been there if he had cut the man's throat. She relaxed. So he had kept his word and not killed the man.

Fortune climbed into the car. "Take us to this club, Ronald."

"You got it, boss."

A blood freezing scream now ripped through the night, from the Hornsby house. A scream that Tais shockingly realized came from Paulie's throat. She looked at Fortune with an expression that might have been fear. He did not look at her as he settled back in the seat.

The Cadillac roared off into the night.

───── ∞∞∞ ─────

The Choco Club, located in Sovereign City's downtown, looked as if it were doing brisk business. The valets were busy hopping in and out of long luxury cars, parking them in the lot located across the street. The line waiting to get in stretched down to the corner.

"Drive by slowly, Ronald." Fortune ordered. Ronald nodded and did so.

Fortune and Tais both ran expert, professional eyes over the brilliantly lit front of the club. He half turned to Tais. "You think she's there?"

Tais shrugged. "I think it's a good chance. I took care that the press didn't get word of Hornsby's murder. Could be Miss Cole hasn't heard about it yet. Therefore there's no reason for her to jackrabbit. What's the play?"

"You go on in right through the front. Ask to speak to Miss Cole if she's there."

"What about you?"

"Oh, I'll be inside. You just go on. I will see you inside the club."

Ronald stopped the Cadillac long enough for Tais to hop out. She delicately half-ran across the street, dodging the slow moving traffic until reaching the door of the club. Fortune saw her whisper in the ear of one of the two bouncers/doormen. The man grinned as Tais pressed bills into his hand. He waved her on inside.

"She's in. Go down the street a bit, then turn about and come back up on that side."

Ronald obliged. Fortune had spied an alley next to The Choco Club that he surmised led to the rear of the establishment. He instructed Ronald to pull up near the alley. "Stay here. Keep the motor running. But this time, if you hear any disturbance inside, don't come in to help. If things go wrong inside, Tais and I will need to get away quick and that is your job. Clear?"

"Understood, Boss. Be careful."

Fortune gave Ronald a reassuring pat on the shoulder and left the car, striding down the dark alley. Just as he figured, it led to the rear of The Choco Club. Standing just outside the service entrance were three black men, two wearing waiter's uniforms, the other a dirty apron and a paper cap askew on the top of his head. They paused in their cigarette smoking, eyeing Fortune warily.

"Good evening, brothers," Fortune said in greeting. "Busy inside?"

The three men's eyes narrowed in suspicion as they took in Fortune's attire. He had never changed out of the tuxedo he wore on his ship and that, along with his stylish duster, fedora and gloves spoke more loudly to the three men than any words.

One of the waiters snarled, "Goan an' get yo' black ass outta here, man. You know full well this here's a white club. You best to be gettin' on back uptown where you belong."

"You misunderstand me, brothers. I'm not looking for trouble but I do need to get inside the club." Fortune held up his platinum money clip. "I will make it worth your while."

The man in the apron suddenly exclaimed, "Hey! I know who you are!" He turned to his co-workers. "This here's Fortune McCall!"

That name instantly changed the attitude of the waiters. "You're the cat what owns that fancy gamblin' ship? Well, shit, why didn't you say so?" They held out their hands to be shaken, which Fortune did gladly.

"What'choo doin' 'round here, Fortune?"

"Looking for the singer, Wilma Cole. Is she inside?"

One of the waiters shook his head in a negative, dropping his cigarette butt on the ground and grinding it out with a heel. "Nah. She be late. An' the boss be raisin' holy hell. But you ain't got to go sneakin' 'round back here to get inside, Fortune. Hell, you just about one of the half dozen a' us in this town who can walk into white folk's joints through the front door without gettin' shot."

"I need to get inside without anybody knowing it's me. And I need your help to do so."

The three men swapped glances and it was the man with the apron who spoke for all of them, "What'choo need, Fortune?"

"Not much at all. Let me explain…"

———⋘⋙———

Tais stood for a minute next to the bar, getting the layout of the place, noting exits and the men stationed around the lavishly huge combination dining room/dance hall. Men who even though they wore tuxedoes were obvious to her trained eye were just ready for trouble. They all were armed. Oh well, best to charge straight on in and get this over with.

Tais walked across the dance floor, nimbly weaving her way around the enthusiastically cha-cha-cha'ing dancers. The reason why the place was named The Choco Club was apparent from the chocolate and cream color design of the club, even to the tuxedoes the twelve piece band wore.

Tais put on her most disarming, sweetest smile and said to the hard-eyed tough giving her the one over, "Hiya, honey. Wilma here?"

"Who wants ta know?"

"I got some money for her. She told me to meet her here."

The tough cocked his head to the side. "Yeah? How much money?"

"What business is it of yours? Look, is Wilma here or not? I'm a busy woman and I have places to be."

"Come on back with me." The tough led the way as they navigated to the rear of the club. They walked halfway down the long corridor lined with doors on both side until coming to the end. The tough knocked on the door.

"Who is it?"

"Spinsy. I got a dame here says she got some dough for Wilma."

"C'mon in!"

Spinsy opened the door and motioned for Tais to walk on in. Two men occupied the office. The one sitting on the desk with the huge black .45 automatic held loosely in his right hand looked miserable. The man sitting tied to the armchair, his face battered into a bloody mess looked considerably even more miserable.

"Come on in, sweet stuff. Spinsy, close that door and get her bag."

Tais mentally cursed herself for walking into such a mess. This was the second time tonight she'd been caught flat-footed and there might not be a third time if she didn't get on the ball. Time to pull the helpless waif routine. She put on her best goopy doe-eyed look and whined, "Say, what's all this about? I didn't come here lookin' for no trouble! I just wanted to see Wilma!"

"Kwitcher lyin', skirt. You ain't no friend a'Wilma's."

"And who arc you?"

The man with the gun smiled. It was a smile that did nothing to ease Tais' mind. "Dominick Cappellano. Ring any bells?"

It certainly did. Dominick Cappellano bossed the most notorious and vicious bootlegging gang in Sovereign City. He'd risen to the top in a very simple way: he killed the competition. No negotiation. No parley. No brokering of terms. You either worked for or kicked up to Cappellano or you got a bullet in the head.

"Hey, Dom…get a load'a this." Spinsy tossed over a billfold he'd taken from Tais' handbag. "And look what she's packin'" he held up her .45.

Cappellano held up his own .45 in salute. "You got good taste in guns, sweet stuff." He looked at the billfold. "Well, well, well…we got us a Special Deputy of The Office of The Mayor of Sovereign City here, Spinsy. You one'a them do-gooders The Mayor's got runnin' around the city? You got a fancy name as well?"

"My name is Tais Pennington-Smythe."

"Not as catchy as Machine McQueen or Aura O'Neal, but it's yours so you gotta live with it. What's your interest in Wilma?"

"Guess there's no point in lying. I represent the rightful owners of the gold you're undoubtedly looking for. I intend to get it."

"She got spine, don't she, Dom?" Spinsy chuckled from his post at the door. Tais accurately pinpointed his position from the sound of his voice.

"She does at that. We don't know where the gold is, sweet stuff. Thought this boy did but he don't talk so easy."

"And who is he?"

"Macklin. The club's owner. I'm trying to find out where Wilma is but he's not inclined to tell us. He's gonna force me to start cutting his toes off."

A light bulb went off in Tais' brain. "The gunsels in the club…your boys?"

Cappellano nodded. "Macklin's boys are locked up in the basement."

"You didn't kill them?"

"Nah. Usually I would'a. But we don't got the time to be cleanin' up that many bodies tonight."

"Just out of curiosity…how did you hear about the gold?"

Cappellano's smile widened. "You don't know? Didn't you question Hornsby's assistant?"

"What's he got to do with this?"

"Sweet stuff, he's got everything to do with this. He went around selling the info to anybody who'd put a thousand bucks in his hand. There must be at least a dozen gangs running around right now looking for that gold. Including my mob. You wanna throw in with me? I'll cut you in for ten…no, let's make it twenty thousand if you do."

"Why so generous?"

"Because them that get greedy are gonna end up with nothing. I'm ruthless but I ain't greedy. And I'm a straight shooter. You play ball with me, I play ball with you."

A polite rapping on the door brought everybody's head around. Even Macklin, who seemed to be regaining slightly. The front of his shirt was no longer white. Blood from his lips and nose dripped onto it.

Spinsy called out, "Who is it?"

"I'se here wit yo' drinks from the bar, suh."

Spinsy cocked a suspicious eye at his boss. "I didn't order drinks. Did you?"

"No. But what the hell. I could use a stiff one and Macklin don't have any booze in here. What's the chances of a club owner what don't have a bar in his office? Let him in."

Spinsy obliged and a waiter shuffled on in, bearing a tray with two drinks. "The barman told me to bring these on in, suh."

"Well bring it on over here, willya? I'm dyin' for a drink."

The waiter crossed the office in three steps. He didn't seem to hurry or move fast but he covered the ground in three heartbeats. The metal tray slammed into Cappellano's face while the waiter's right hand went out to seize Cappellano's gun hand. The waiter forced the gun down as a bullet whined into the floor.

Tais whirled around, putting the momentum of her spin into a roundhouse punch that took Spinsy flush in the jaw, lifting him up completely off his feet. He slammed into the door and slid to the floor, out cold.

The waiter finished up Cappellano with a sharp uppercut that threw the bootlegger over the desk to collapse on the floor behind it in a loose–limbed heap.

Tais glared at Fortune McCall. "You sure took your time about getting in here! And what's with the waiter getup?"

"I thought it best I infiltrate the club without anybody knowing it was me. And in this culture, a Negro wearing a waiter's uniform or pushing a broom is totally invisible. As you can see, it paid off. Who's this unfortunate gentleman?"

Fortune gestured at the bound man in the chair who was looking at Fortune and Tais with something akin to groggy amazement.

"Macklin. He's the club's owner. He may know where Wilma Cole is."

Fortune reached into a hidden sheath and drew forth a slim blade, giving it hilt first to Tais. "Cut him loose while I tie up these men." Fortune bent to his task, using their own belts to secure them while Tais cut the ropes around Macklin's arms and legs binding him to the chair.

"I don't know how we're going to get out of here, Fortune. The guy you clocked is Dom Cappellano."

"The bootlegger? How did he get mixed up in this caper?"

"Apparently things have become more complicated."

"Well, of course they have."

⸺∞⸺

Tracy Scott and Eddie Padilla pulled up to Hornsby's decoy home in a Cadillac that was twin to the one Fortune and Ronald were using. A number of police cars were parked in front of the house. And what looked to be a small army of policemen milled inside and out. Tracy and Eddie swapped worried looks as they climbed out of the car and went on in the house.

Chief Lawrence Tate spied them immediately and waved them on over to him.

"Want you to know we appreciate your contacting us, Chief," Eddie said feelingly. "Mr. McCall will appreciate it as well."

"You can save it, Padilla. You want to show me your appreciation, you find me McCall and you tell him to come see me. Take a look at this." Tate jerked his chin at two bodies covered by a blood soaked sheet. Tracy walked over, flipped back the sheet, and ran her expert eye over the bodies.

"You've got two dead men here."

"Wrong. What I've got is two white men shotgunned to death. I got a live white man with a blown-off kneecap who gave a pretty good description of the man who he says killed those two. And since I know that McCall favors a sawed-off Browning A-5, what we got here is a mess."

"I'm sure if Mr. McCall killed these men, they had it coming to them," Eddie said calmly.

"Look, Padilla, far as I'm concerned, as long as McCall shoots trash like this that won't be missed, I don't care what color they are. Yellow, white, black or brown, it don't make me no never mind. But what I do mind is not being kept informed as to what McCall is doing or why. Because there's a lot of powerful folks in this city who don't like the idea of a colored man going around shooting white men. Even hoods like these two. I can't cover for him if I don't know what's going on."

Eddie held up his hands in surrender, "Chief Tate, you've got my word of honor that we have no idea what Mr. McCall is doing. Matter of fact, Miss Scott and I are trying to find him our ownselves. The last thing we heard, he was with our associate Mr. Scocco and Miss Pennington-Smythe."

Chief Tate grunted. "The British spy lady. Okay, now this starting to come together."

"What do you mean, Chief?"

"Some British banker was murdered earlier this evening. Your Miss Pennington-Smythe took charge of the investigation. Asked us to stay out of it. She brought in her own people to secure the crime scene and everything. Made sure it didn't get into the papers."

Eddie and Tracy swapped extremely puzzled looks. "What is the world is Fortune doing getting mixed up with a murdered British banker?" Tracy wondered aloud.

Chief Tate pointed a finger at Eddie. "I'm holding you responsible,

Padilla. You're McCall's lawyer so I'm putting you on notice. I want McCall in my office in twenty-four hours to explain this. After that, I'll have no choice but to issue a warrant for his arrest."

Tracy started to protest but Eddie caught her eye and signaled that she should hold her tongue. To Chief Tate, Eddie merely said, "Fair enough, Chief. We'll find him."

Chief Tate grunted in satisfaction and walked away. Tracy hissed, "Why did you agree to that?"

"Because Tate's okay. The man's just covering his own ass and I can't blame him for that. And neither would Fortune. Tate's giving us enough time to find Fortune on our own and that's just what we're going to do. There's got to be a phone in here somewhere. We're going to start calling all our contacts and find out where Fortune's been tonight. Somebody has to have seen him." Eddie looked back down at the two dead bodies. "Hopefully somebody who's still alive."

Macklin emerged from the small rest room adjacent to his office. Now that he had washed his face, he looked somewhat better. It would take days for the swelling to go down, though. Cappellano had been viciously thorough in his beating of the man.

"Wanna thank the two of you for gettin' me outta that fix," Macklin mumbled through swollen lips.

"If you want to thank us, tell us where Wilma Cole is," Fortune suggested.

"I'll do better than that. I'll take you to her. C'mon."

Fortune threw a glance at Cappellano and Spinsy. They were both still out cold and securely bound. He turned back to Macklin and indicated he should lead the way.

Macklin walked over to what appeared to be a solid wall. He placed his hand on the wall, held it there for maybe twenty seconds. He took it away and again placed it on the same spot. A hidden door in the wall swung inwards, revealing a flight of well-lit stairs leading down.

Fortune nodded in admiration as he and Tais followed Macklin. "Ingenious. The door is opened by the heat of your hand. There's no lock to pick or hidden switch to trip."

Macklin's head turned and he threw Fortune a quick grin. "Cost me a lotta jake to have it hooked up like that but it's worth it. Close that door, willya?"

Fortune did so and they continued downwards until coming to a comfortable little hidden apartment. A fairly sized living room, kitchen, and bedroom. It also contained Wilma Cole. The singer sat in a chair, drinking a Scotch and water, listening to the music being played above her head thanks to a Philips radio. Her eyes opened as wide as they could possibly get as she slowly stood up, the chunky glass slipping out of her hand to land with a dull thud to the carpeted floor. She had platinum hair similar to Tais. But where Tais had pure platinum hair, Wilma's had gold highlights. Her silver evening dress fit her so tightly that she might well have been sewn into it.

"Mack? Who are they? What's going on?"

"Look here, baby, we got to talk. Things have changed." Macklin gently took her by the hand and sat her down and in a brief two minutes explained how Cappellano had taken over his club and brutally beaten him to try and make him talk. "If it hadn't been for the two of them-" he jerked his head in the general direction of Fortune and Tais, "-I'd be a dead man."

"But who are they?"

"Well, I heard her call him Fortune so I'd say he's Fortune McCall, the guy what operates the gambling ship. And with that limey accent of hers, she's gotta be that English girl workin' for the Mayor's Office."

"I work with Mayor Byles. Not for him. And my name is Tais Pennington-Smythe. I'm here on behalf of the British government." Tais fixed Wilma with her best blood-freezing stare. "And you're in quite the hot soup, my dear. So hot it's scalding. You and your boyfriend stole a considerable sum of money from my government and I intend to get it back."

Wilma's huge eyes went from Tais, to Macklin and finally to Fortune. "I didn't know anybody was going to get killed!" she wailed helplessly. "Mack, tell them! This was all your fault!"

Fortune and Tais swapped looks before turning their mutual suspicious gazes on Macklin. "Care to explain that one, Mr. Macklin?" Fortune asked quietly.

Macklin spoke rapidly, his hands spread out as if begging for alms. "Look, it was Hornsby's own fault! He started braggin' to Wilma about how he was stealin' a lot of money for the two of them to go away together. I suggested...and mind you it was only a suggestion that she vamp the limey and find out where the money was! Then we'd lift it and leg it on outta this burg, leave Hornsby to take the rap!"

"Wait just a bloody minute!" Tais pointed a long finger at Wilma. "So you weren't shacking up with Hornsby?"

"Well…yes…but only to find out where the money was! I'm with Mack! Everybody knows that!"

Fortune laughed softly. "Are there no honest thieves in the world any more?" He looked at Tais, shaking his head slowly in dismay. "Your banker double crosses Box 850 and steals from them for this woman who he thought was in love with him. But she double crosses him for the love of this man who thinks nothing of pimping out his woman to lay his hands on the money. And in the meantime, Hornsby's trusted assistant sells him out to every criminal gang in the city." Fortune's laughter got louder. "And by the way, Miss Cole…did it at any time occur to you that your paramour there may just have been planning to leave you and make off with all the gold by himself?"

Wilma threw her arms around Macklin's neck. "Mack wouldn't do that! Would you, baby?"

"'Course, not! He's just talkin' 'cause he likes the sound a' his voice!" But the look in Macklin's eyes said more eloquently than any words that Fortune had hit the spot.

"Whatever you two had planned, it's over as of now. I want that gold and I want it now."

"You're welcome to it," Macklin said feelingly. He gingerly touched his swollen face. "Look, I ain't no tough guy. I run a nightclub and that's it. Sure, I saw a chance to make some big dough and I took it." He shrugged. "Who wouldn't? But I didn't know guys like Dom Cappellano were in the game. He plays too rough for me." Macklin looked at Fortune. "And from what I hear, you ain't no pushover, either."

"My friend will be the least of your problems, Mr. Macklin. I can promise you that. Now, where the hell is that gold?" Tais said firmly.

Macklin stood up, Wilma still hanging onto his neck. "I'll take you to it."

"How do we get out of here without being seen?"

Macklin jerked a thumb over his shoulder. "When I bought this club and built this hideout down here, I also bought the building next door. There's a tunnel that goes there. We can get out without having to go through the club. C'mon."

Tracy hung up the phone and hurried from the Hornsby bedroom to find Eddie outside talking to Chief Tate. "Okay, we've got something. Fortune, Tais, and Ronald stopped at Honeychile's for eats. They left from there and somebody said they saw his vehicle over by The Choco Club. I called up the club, asked to speak to the head waiter who confirms that Fortune is there."

Chief Tate said crisply, "I'll send a couple of cars and a half dozen of my lads with you!"

"I wish you wouldn't, Chief," Eddie said. "We don't know what the situation is and pulling up to the club with a crew of police officers may make the situation worse. May even get somebody killed. Let me and Tracy go by ourselves and scout the situation out."

"Okay, I'll play along for now. I know you've got radiophones in your cars. You get back to me in an hour and let me know what's going on!"

"My word on it. Tracy, let's go!"

Ronald Scocco nimbly climbed out of the car and quickly opened the passenger door. Fortune, Tais, Wilma, and Macklin piled in. He slammed the door shut, ran around to the driver's side, jumped in, and pulled away from the curb quickly but without a screeching of tires that would have drawn attention.

Fortune made the introductions, "Ronald, this is Miss Cole and Mr. Macklin. They're going to be taking us to the gold so follow their directions if you please."

"Anything you say, Boss. I've got your coat, hat and gloves here in the front seat. A waiter from the club brought them out to me."

"Excellent. And now, Miss Cole? Where is the gold?"

For the first time since they had met her, Wilma Cole smiled. "Where's the best place to hide a needle?"

"In a haystack. Everybody knows that," Ronald replied.

Fortune snapped his fingers. "No. The best place to hide a needle is in a box with other needles."

"Oh my God," Tais whispered in sudden understanding. "The

Federal Reserve Bank of Sovereign City. That magnificently sneaky bastard!"

Fortune nodded. "We simply assumed that he had the money he embezzled converted into gold and then he hid it someplace. Why go through all that bother when he could simply put the excess gold in with the bullion already stored there? I'm sure that he was provided with the protocols necessary to accomplish this, am I right?"

Tais nodded. "It's a good thing for Hornsby that he's already dead otherwise I'd kill him myself!"

"But we can't get into The Federal Reserve Bank in the middle of the night, Miss Cole," Fortune said. "So where are we going?"

"Herbie changed all the protocols. If you don't know what they are, you'll never get that gold. He had it fixed so that if anything happened to him before he could get it out, it would be spread out among a dozen different accounts in a dozen different cities. And not just the gold he stole. All the British gold in their vault would be spread out."

Tais gasped, "Fortune, we have got to get those new protocols. You can't imagine how much gold is in that vault."

"Oh, I have a good imagination and I can image quite a lot. We-"

And that's when the Willys sedan slammed into the Cadillac from the rear. Fortune and the others in the rear seat were tossed to and fro as the Willys surged forward and smashed into the Cadillac's rear again and yet again. Ronald controlled the car with a skill and surety beyond his young years. The bone jangling impacts would have thrown the car to one side of the street or the other in an out-of-control skid if Ronald did not know what he was doing.

The boy kept the Cadillac in a straight line, rocketing down the street, weaving in and around the slower moving traffic. He kept his left hand on the steering wheel and with the right reached down for Fortune's shotgun. He passed it back to its owner's waiting hands. Ronald then pressed a button on the dashboard and the rear window obligingly slid down and out of the way, thus eliminating the inconvenience of Fortune having to shoot out the glass.

The shotgun whoomed, taking out the left headlight of the Willys. Fortune's next two shots were placed squarely in the engine. Steam erupted in thick geysers from the ruptures. The driver of the Willys, unable to see, twisted the wheel in panic, hit a fire hydrant. Water gushed not only into the vehicle but out on all sides, drenching fleeing pedestrians and flooding the street.

Ronald hung a screeching right on the two right wheels and continued on.

"Everybody okay?" Fortune asked calmly.

"Like I said, you boys play way too rough for me," Macklin grumbled. He and Wilma sat with their arms wrapped around each other. Wilma appeared to have lost the power to speak, so frightened was she.

Another long, low slung sedan of European make roared out of a side alley, heading straight at the Cadillac. Machine gun fire howled from the rolled down windows, echoing up and down the street. Bullets harmlessly spanged off the side of Fortune's car with no effect other than scratching the paint job. All of Fortune's vehicles were bullet proofed.

Tais snarled, "Okay, that's enough!" She threw open the door and leaned out, hanging onto the door with one hand while blasting away with her .45 automatic. Her accurately placed shots blew out the front two tires. The sedan flipped up and over, performing two complete somersaults before crashing back down to earth with a deafening cacophony of crushing metal and shattering glass.

Fortune yanked her back inside the car, the door slamming shut.

"You do know you could have fallen out performing that stunt?"

Tais grinned at him as she replaced the spent clip with a fresh one. "Oh, you wouldn't have let anything happen to me. You haven't gotten your ten percent yet!"

———— ∞ ————

Ronald cautiously turned the corner, turning off the Cadillac's headlights. "Didn't think I'd be back here again tonight," he chuckled.

He referred to the fact that once again they were approaching the second Hornsby house where just a few short hours ago Fortune, Tais, and Ronald had been in desperate combat against a gang of killers. The police were gone by now. They'd taken the dead bodies, boarded up the doors, and departed.

"Ronald, you can park here in the driveway," Fortune ordered. "This isn't going to take long so you can come on in with us if you like."

They all climbed out of the car. Between Fortune and Macklin, it was the work of two minutes to rip the boards off the front door and enter the Hornsby home.

Wilma held up her dress so that she would not trip on the hem and gingerly walked on her stiletto heels over to the piano and picked up the silver framed photograph of herself and Hornsby. She opened the frame and slid the photo out. She handed it to Tais.

Tais read the information written on the back and looked up at Fortune with relief brightening her face. "It's all here. I can separate the gold Hornsby stole from the gold that is already in the vault."

"Or what say we just help ourselves to the whole boodle?" The new voice belonged to a beefy customer who stepped through the front door. Five more men crowded in behind him, spreading out so as to cover Fortune and the others.

Fortune sighed. "And who might you be?"

"Names Sheffield. I've had my men following you two all night. I figured if I'd just be patient you'd lead me to the information."

"Let me guess: you purchased the information about the gold from Hornsby's assistant."

"Nah! I run a half dozen boats in and out of Sovereign. You want something smuggled in or out, I'm your boy. Hornsby hired me to take him and some girl out of Sovereign. After I heard about the gold it wasn't hard to connect up the dots. Now…pass over that photo, lady!"

"I don't think so," Fortune said quietly. "In fact, I think you should drop your guns and surrender."

Sheffield laughed. "Surrender to who? You?"

"No," said a firm voice from behind Sheffield. A voice belonging to Chief Tate. "To me."

More police officers appeared from the rear and kicked in the windows. There had to be at least fifty guns trained on Sheffield and his men.

"You got five seconds to drop those guns before my boys open fire and drop you."

Sheffield shrugged. His revolver thudded to the ground. "Okay, boys, the jig's up. Let's go quietly."

As the crooks were rounded up, an enraged Tracy ran into the house and punched Fortune solidly in the chest. "I ought to kill you!"

"Good to see you, too, cousin," Fortune replied soberly, rubbing the spot she had hit. He didn't mention how much it hurt. Tracy could have hit a lot harder than that. Hard enough to break the breastbone, in fact.

Eddie joined them, pushing back his hat and standing with his hands on his hips. "Y'know, I got better things to do than chase all over this city looking for you. Just what the hell have you three been up to all night?"

Fortune wrapped his arms around Eddie and Tracy. "Let's go get breakfast with Chief Tate and I can explain the whole thing to everybody at one time. Oh, just a moment." Fortune turned to cock an eye at Tais. "Our deal still holds?"

"Of course. If I'm included in that breakfast."

"But of course you are." Fortune stepped outside and looked as the first hint of dawn tinged the impressive skyline of Sovereign City. He took a deep breath. "I do think it's going to be a beautiful day, don't you?"

⸻

Back at Honeychile's everybody enjoyed their breakfast while Fortune and Tais explained the extraordinary events of the previous night. Chief Tate forked down sausage and eggs with one hand while the other hand took notes. "I think I got enough to satisfy the press. I can get the mayor to put pressure on the press and minimize your participation in this business, McCall."

"I'm obliged, Chief."

"I still don't understand why you didn't call us in for help," Tracy snapped. "With us on the job we could have found that gold in half the time!"

"And thereby depriving me of half my fun." Fortune sighed and picked up his coffee cup. "Every so often I wonder if I'm depending on you, Eddie and the others a bit too much. It's good for me to test myself and make sure I'm not losing my edge."

"Oh, you ain't gonna do that," Tracy grinned wickedly. "Until further notice your workouts are gonna be four hours instead of two."

"Ouch," Fortune said mildly. "I suppose I deserve that. And a little extra sweat wouldn't hurt."

A Sovereign City police officer ran inside the restaurant and whispered in Tate's ear. Tate's face wrinkled in alarm. He looked over at Fortune. "You're not going to believe this."

"What happened?"

"Faceless Cabrini just broke out of the Detention House where he was being held awaiting transfer to Denbrook Penitentiary. And get this, the preliminary reports claim he was assisted by pygmies in armor."

"Now that's something you don't hear everyday," Tais said.

Chief Tate hauled his bulk up out of his chair. "Guess I'm on the clock again. Thanks again, Fortune-"

"Hold on just a moment, Chief. I owe my associates a caper and this looks like one they can sink their teeth into."

"Hey, you want it, you can have it."

Fortune picked up his fedora, placed it on his head, and reached for his duster. "Eddie, you contact Regina and Pasquale and ask them to meet us at the Detention House. Stephen's in charge of the ship. Tais, you want in on this?"

Tais put down her coffee cup. "Oh, what the hell…why not?"

They left the restaurant in a rush and piled into their two cars. Fortune paused before climbing into the lead car and gave Chief Tate a salute and wink.

"May your day be filled with good fortune, sir." Then he was inside and the car roared off into the new day.

THE END

CPSIA information can be obtained
at www.ICGtesting.com
Printed in the USA
BVHW041256200121
598227BV00018B/338

9 781468 112566